THE DEADLY TRANSIT OF TOBY BARNES

By David T. Snyder

Kleenan Press
Post Office Box 1213
Walled Lake, Michigan 48390

Library of Congress Control Number 2007903054

Printed in the United States of America

ISBN 978-0-9745081-3-9

To my mother, whose optimistic

assessment of my capacities was

flattering but entirely unrealistic.

Chapter One

Donny Leroy Scroggins had driven the stolen Dodge pickup to its limits on one of the rare straight-aways along a two-lane stretch of Ozark highway as his twin brother, Leroy Donny, slouched in the passenger seat, a newly lit Marlborough dangling from his lips and two single-barreled shotguns propped against one leg. It was early afternoon on a flawless fall day and the brothers were in an uncharacteristically good mood as they approached the outskirts of Stockton, their immediate destination. They had earlier that day robbed a small convenience store and murdered the elderly proprietor for no apparent reason.

"Did you see the look on that old fart's face," Leroy Donny said as his brother eased off the accelerator when they passed a series of dispersed houses that were the first indicators of the approaching community. "I don't think he expected to die just yet." Donny Leroy ignored him, more concerned with finding the Blanchard County Bank and Trust Company they intended to rob as pay-back for the 18 years their father, Calvin, had spent in the state penitentiary before his recent death of reasonably natural causes. The bank was within the jurisdiction of Sheriff Jesse Jones, who had arrested Calvin in the murder of another man and who still held office and enforced law in the county with a firm but enlightened hand.

Donny Leroy and Leroy Donny were fraternal rather than identical twins and bore little physical resemblance to one another, although their limited intelligence, twangy speech and dirty, worn jeans were quite similar. Not recently washed, Donny's long, dark hair clung consistently to his head, unruffled by the rush of air through the side window. Large orange lettering on the back of his black tee shirt, both faded, said "Kick Ass," a contrast to Leroy's plain white shirt that said nothing at all. Donny continued the truck's deceleration in deference to the gathering town and peered intently through the windshield, unaware of the differing economic and social statements made by the various neighborhoods that swept past his view. Leroy, who had shot the old man for amusement, was equally indifferent to the emerging real estate.

"The eighty-two dollars we got out of that cash drawer was hardly worth the ammunition, he said. "The morning would have been a total loss if I hadn't whacked that geezer." An accumulated ash from his cigarette fell into his lap, dislodged by his moving lips. His brother continued to ignore him, intent on finding the inevitable sign that would reveal direction to the main business district where the bank, he accurately assumed, did business. Stockton's modest downtown area had remained viable, mostly because the community was too small to attract one of the international retailers whose mammoth stores – generally built on the population outskirts – sucked commercial life out of the old central districts.

The twins were eight years old when their father shot his best friend to death. He caught the man, buck naked, between the elevated legs of his wife and mother of his sons. The shotgun blast from behind removed a substantial part of the former friend's skull, but the wife, mainly shielded by the victim's body, was struck only by miscellaneous buckshot in places that were neither lethal nor cosmetically damaging over the long term. Calvin Scroggins had meant to shoot his wife, but had fetched his gun in a rage and not thought to gather additional shells for the weapon. Although splattered with her lover's blood and oblivious to the buckshot that had peppered the exposed parts of her body, she managed to dislodge herself from under the corpse and flee the trailer home before her husband could reload and find her. She fled into a nearby wood and remained there until the police – called apparently by neighbors – cornered Calvin and disarmed him. She was found soon afterward, hiding naked in the woods where she contracted a severe case of poison ivy to compound the discomfort from her buckshot wounds.

The twins, who had been awakened by their father's rampage through the small trailer, witnessed everything except the actual shooting. At the time, they were too young to understand the nature of their mother's transgression, but they had always been closer to their father. He loved his sons and very little else while she had been mainly indifferent to them, lacking anything that would remotely resemble a maternal instinct. As the twins grew older and came to recognize the reason their father was missing from their lives, their early and reciprocal indifference to the mother gradually developed into something between unspoken dislike and hatred. Her conduct over the remaining years of their boyhoods and teen years – which consisted of one lascivious and drunken episode after another – did little to improve the situation.

The boys, meanwhile, went largely unsupervised and were left with their rather limited capacities to blunder into one mischief after another, beginning with petty theft and, later, culminating in a long series of felonies. They had dropped out of school early, unnoticed by the authorities, and had commenced undistinguished criminal careers to get pocket money by any means short of work. Through miraculous luck, the brothers managed to avoid arrest for a multitude of petty and a few grand thefts, and were only captured and sent to a juvenile correctional facility when they attempted to rob an off-duty deputy sheriff with a water pistol they thought resembled the real thing. The deputy knew a water pistol when he saw one, and used his own real weapon to restrain the twins, who were somewhere in their mid-teens at the time.

Donny had little difficulty finding the business district and the bank, but parking was another matter. "Crap," he muttered, mostly to himself, realizing he needed to find a space reasonably close to the bank if they were to rob the place and make a clean get-away. "Do you see anything?" he asked his brother, assuming Leroy knew what he was talking about.

"Huh?" Leroy said, intent on retrieving a handful of double aught shotgun shells from the glove box where he had stowed them earlier that day.

"A parking spot, goddammit," Donny replied. "Do you see a parking spot?" As he spoke, a small sedan pulled out of a space only a few yards from the bank entrance, and Donny pulled the truck into it, cutting off another car whose driver, an elderly woman, had been waiting ahead of him for the spot. "Did you see the look on her face?" Leroy asked as he loaded the two guns and handed a few shells to his brother. "That's one pissed old lady," he added, dispersing the remaining shells between his shirt and rear pants pockets.

The brothers – who spent several years in the juvenile correctional facility – were released to the custody of their mother, who only accepted the responsibility with the provision, agreed to between them, that they contribute to her support. They subsequently moved into a trailer in the same park where she still lived, and remained there until her continuing complaints about their failure to honor the money agreement drove them to even seedier digs in a two room apartment over an old pool hall. They lived together mostly out of habit rather than affection, and because their increasingly criminal conduct developed into something of a partnership arrangement.

Donny and Leroy originally made a subsistence living stealing anything they could sell or trade, eventually working their way up the criminal food chain, but not very far, to Grand Theft Auto. They had gained rudimentary mechanical skills at the correctional facility and employed that knowledge to disassemble their stolen cars for the valuable parts. Working in a small, out-of-the-way shed they rented for thirty dollars a month, they soon developed modestly respectable incomes they spent mainly but not exclusively on beer and pot. They also began to subsidize their father at the state penitentiary, supplying him with pocket money, cigarettes and other minor extravagances. They even visited him with some regularity, but their time together was marked mainly by long silences in which none of them knew what to say. Their original bond had long since been broken, although it was the only one each of them had and they were reluctant to acknowledge its loss. Clinging as they did to this illusion, the twins – who had heard their father's bitter denunciations of the wife who had betrayed him and the sheriff, Jesse Jones, who had brought him down -- became a conduit for the older man's repressed hostilities. And when the older man died unexpectedly, the boys decided to exact revenge in his name on the unfaithful wife, their mother, and the sheriff.

In an almost transcendental coincidence, the twins caught their mother in the same position she had assumed on the night their father shot her lover. But the final result this time was quite different. Donny kicked in the flimsy trailer door and the two sons entered, both with single barreled shotguns.

"Get your naked ass out of here," Donny demanded, and the man, fear-stricken, fled the premises much as their mother had done 18 years earlier. She, meanwhile, sat up in the small bed and glared at them, probably unaware of their intentions and instantaneously surprised when the single blast from Donny's shotgun sent her to eternal oblivion. "Damn," Leroy said as they left the trailer where they had lived as youngsters. "What next?"

Donny, who was the first-born twin, said he thought robbing the bank in the sheriff's hometown would be a good start, but they first needed spare cash against the possibility the bank robbery failed. They needed, he said, to conduct a small robbery to finance the bigger one. He discarded the concept when the convenience store produced so little money, and the brothers, assuming the bank would soon supplement their dwindling funds, headed directly for Stockton. Leroy, who had tasted blood for the first time when he shot the old proprietor, was eager to repeat the experience and thought the bank would provide the next opportunity.

The brothers – both wearing dark wool ski masks in the warm, fall weather – burst into the modest bank lobby to find only a handful of people, among them the bank manager, two tellers and several customers. "This is a stick-up, goddammit," Donny announced in a loud voice, brandishing his shotgun in a sweeping arc that took in everyone before him. Leroy let his twin do the talking, standing behind him and to one side seeking justification – a threatening move – to shoot someone else that same day.

Donny, who was about to order everyone down to the floor, immediately noticed a very large man – not heavy, just large – who carried a worn, leather satchel. "What's in the bag?" the dominant twin demanded.

"Money," the large man replied. "Cash money."

"Let's see," the robber ordered, motioning for the case to be opened. The man obliged, but in an instant produced a substantial handgun he instantly used to shoot Donny through the heart at short range. Leroy – caught entirely by surprise – was leveling his own weapon when the man's second shot struck his forehead, splashing various materials over the white tile floor and a nearby depositor. The shooter, one of the tellers later recalled, prudently kicked the weapons away from the dead bodies, both awkwardly sprawled on their backs. Donny, when his mask was removed, had an expression of incredible disbelief on his face.

Jake Pritchard shot the twins with the cool precision he brought to all his enterprises. A newcomer to the rock-strewn Ozark hills, he had early on attracted the attention of his neighbors by the sheer audacity of those enterprises and an effort – which the locals admired – to keep to himself. Pritchard had acquired and consolidated large, connected parcels of land into a ranch where he had installed a herd of polled Hereford cattle and overseen construction of his own home and numerous outbuildings, all within a matter of months rather than years. That part of his land that fronted on a well-paved state road was set off by an expensive brown and white fence that extended for miles and clearly proclaimed the extent of his holdings.

Although new to the area and restrained in his dealings with strangers, he had soon proven himself a generous benefactor to the community. He had volunteered his own services and those of his ranch hands to sandbag the banks of the Fungus River that ran through the heart of Stockton. Normally placid, the stream had gone on a rampage following weeks of heavy spring rain. Pritchard had also made anonymous cash contributions to a variety of local charities and needy individuals, but his anonymity, while greatly respected, was almost impossible to ensure in a community where very little remained secret for long. That was particularly true when he elected to fly a desperately ill child to a distant medical facility in the small twin-engine plane that was compatible with the ranch's 3,000-foot runway. The charitable act disclosed to everyone in the area that he not only had a plane he could fly but had constructed a paved runway in the interior of his property.

Pritchard's performance at the bank – particularly his obvious skill with firearms – was an initial surprise to those who had met him, but on reflection many decided it was really no surprise at all. They had surmised by his bearing, manner and general appearance – large bodied, muscular with ramrod posture and prematurely graying hair, cut short – that he had done military service. They also speculated on his woman friend, Isabella, and his ranch manager, Diego, but their conjectures came to very little. Pritchard and those close to him remained mainly mysteries to everyone in that remote area that knew them, with one exception.

Sheriff Jesse Jones came to know Pritchard through a variety of circumstances and decided early on to like the taciturn newcomer. He appreciated his generous contributions to the community, respected his polite standoffishness and particularly admired his handling of the bank robbers who, he knew, could well have murdered innocent citizens in the bank that day. He initially knew Pritchard through personal contacts, including his investigation of the robbery and their joint efforts in transporting the stricken child to the medical center. Later and after Pritchard and those close to him had clandestinely deserted the area, the sheriff learned a good deal more from a city detective investigating a couple of related homicides. All the additional information, the sheriff eventually realized, only compounded the mystery. It seemed only to reveal how much he didn't know about a man, suspected of murder, that even the veteran city detective had come to respect. Oddly, the detective – who had never met Pritchard – seemed to know him in a deeply personal as well as a factual way. That was the impression, at least, the sheriff had after a long discussion with Bill Price, who had tracked his quarry to Stockton and learned on his arrival in town that Pritchard had managed to dispose of his vast holdings and disappear only a few days earlier.

"It's amazing," Price told Jones when he learned Pritchard was gone, "how a man his size can vanish so quickly and so completely. He's as strong as a bull, almost as big, and as nimble as an acrobat." Price said he thought some of Pritchard's canny alertness derived from his Special Forces training and experience, which had taken him to remote and dangerous military assignments across the globe. But, mainly, he attributed the man's many skills to intelligence, discipline and a single-mindedness that verged on compulsion.

Price – who had traveled to Stockton with his woman friend, Diana Hornbeck, to appear somewhat less conspicuous than a cop traveling alone – told the sheriff that Jake Pritchard was in reality a man named Toby Barnes who, he strongly suspected but couldn't yet prove, had killed two men to avenge the murder many years earlier of his father. Price said the two victims probably deserved killing and, as he learned later, so did the father of Toby Barnes. He eventually discovered that the father, who taught high school in a small town, had probably been shot to death by a young woman he raped, and that the two murdered men – while more than likely innocent of that crime – had escaped punishment for a host of other bad deeds. Barnes, meanwhile, continued under the illusion he had avenged the death of a good man, a virtuous teacher and father he had barely known. Price told the sheriff that Barnes went on to a distinguished, although somewhat mysterious military career, and managed not long after his discharge from service to amass an enormous fortune by means that were even more mysterious than his Army service. Price didn't know that Toby Barnes, who became Jake Pritchard to establish a new life on his Ozark ranch, had planned and executed a daring raid in a Central American jungle on the fortress of an international drug lord, a man with an established reputation for murder and other crimes on a grand scale. With a small detachment of hardened, specifically trained former Special Forces types, inside information he cleverly gained from various sources and a meticulous plan, Barnes destroyed the drug lord, his fortress and, overnight, acquired the vast wealth that had been stored in that remote stronghold as well as access to various off-shore depositories. The extent of that wealth was sufficient to enable him to enrich those who had followed him – intensely loyal men that had seen hard service with him in the regular Army – and provide the means to accomplish almost anything money can buy.

Price was unable to determine the source or the extent of his adversary's wealth, which far exceeded his meager resources. The detective, in fact, had spent his own money and personal vacation time to make the trip to Stockton, unable to get his cash-strapped city department to cover the expense. The cost was not much of a burden to Price, however, who had been modestly successful in the stock market over the years and had recently received several hundred thousand dollars from the estate of an aunt who had taken him in as a teenager on the death of his parents in an automobile accident. He had the means to personally finance parts of an investigation that had acquired personal implications for him, but he soon learned that Barnes or Pritchard had achieved wealth that rivaled the fortunes of the famously rich.

Price began to suspect the extent of Pritchard's wealth when he traced the small, twin-engine plane – whose license number Sheriff Jones had seen when he brought the sick child to the ranch airstrip – and learned it had been traded for an expensive new turbo-prop aircraft, paid for with the former rancher's personal check. The detective then followed a trail that clearly showed money was no obstacle to anything Pritchard sought and one that eventually led to the British Virgin Islands where the fugitive had established another elaborate residence. Price – who by this time had convinced himself for mainly personal reasons that Pritchard's homicides were justifiable or, at least, understandable – remained on the trail like some grizzled old hound whose deep biological instincts left him no alternative. But, again, he arrived in the British Virgins to learn his quarry – now traveling with his woman friend, Isabella, as Mr. and Mrs. Paul Striker – had quietly decamped only a day earlier. The elusive Toby Barnes, Price discovered, had mastered the concept of contingency planning and left for other parts when a state-side associate alerted him to Price's imminent arrival in the tropics. This time his departure left no clue to his next destination and it would be some time before the detective had even an inkling of where he had gone.

Sheriff Jones learned the identity of the two dead robbers when he arrived at the bank shortly after their attempted robbery. He easily recalled their other attempted robbery of his off-duty deputy with a water pistol because it was the kind of event that tends to linger in a law enforcement officer's memory. He also knew the twins were the sons of a man he had long ago sent to prison, and had assumed they were destined for some form of trouble.

The theft of the pick-up truck and two murders in less than 24 hours had put Sheriff Jones on their trail before they arrived at the bank. He had also received a phone call from a witness who reported two armed masked men entering the institution, and he would have been hard on their trail had Pritchard not made the chase unnecessary. Jones told all this to Price during their meeting in Stockton. "This was probably the most incompetent crime wave in the whole history of crime," the sheriff said. "They left a trail even a blind man could follow and their stolen truck, we discovered later, was sitting outside the bank with a dead battery."

*

Chapter Two

Most of the detectives and many of the others assigned to the bureau where Bill Price had worked for more than 20 years suspected he had beaten a homeless junkie to death with his gloved fists. There was no conclusive evidence, only conjecture he had done the crime to avenge the brutal murder of the aunt who had taken him in as an early teenager when his parents died. There was substantial evidence linking the vagrant to the robbery and homicide and there was little doubt Price had motive – he had seen the elderly woman's battered body – and opportunity, but two detectives assigned to investigate the case were unable to prove anything and unwilling to implicate a man whose solid reputation throughout the city's law enforcement community was substantial.

Price had neither the inclination nor the political instincts to achieve commanding rank in the department, but his native intelligence, physical strength and bull-headed tenacity had won the respect of his colleagues and a good deal of deference from principal figures in the local underworld. Those who knew him understood he was honest to the core, but would bend the rules beyond recognition to achieve what he considered justice. The dead junkie, many thought, was simply Price's concept of justice rendered promptly and at small cost to the public.

Other than a four-year Marine Corps hitch where he had been a rifle range instructor at the recruit training base on Parris Island, South Carolina, William Seabrook Price II had been a cop his entire adult life. He had attended a private school and was destined for an Ivy League university before his parents died, but wound up in the public high school where his guardian and aunt was a science teacher and coach of the girl's basketball team. Although he mourned his parents in his own private manner, the change in his academic situation was of small concern to him. He had little interest in a university education and enlisted in the Marine Corps shortly after his high school graduation with respectable but unremarkable grades. He was probably best remembered by contemporary students for his dogged performance as a lineman on the football team, where his early strength and tenacity were notable enough to attract college scouts.

Price had scant interest in an advanced education, but was curious by nature and read widely in those subjects that interested him. He was particularly fond of history, although his preference was for the clear-cut narratives of competent popular historians, writers such as Barbara Tuchman, William Manchester and, particularly, Samuel Eliot Morison whose books combined a knowledge of history and seamanship that the land-locked mid-westerner found compelling. His interest in maritime events led him to an early attachment to Britain's great naval hero, Lord Nelson, who gave his life at Cape Trafalgar in 1805 to save his country from a rapacious French enemy.

Price admired the diminutive Nelson's vast courage, wondering at times how a man so small could lose an eye and an arm in the service of his country and maintain a posture that continued to command enormous respect and service from both his men and the provocative Emma, Lady Hamilton, who became his mistress. His respect for Nelson took on physical form when Price began work on a large, detailed model of the admiral's flagship, Victory, which his friends eventually decided would never come to completion. He worked on it at intervals for years, eventually understanding that satisfaction was in the work and that very little would be accomplished if it were finished. It was the journey that was important and not the destination, as someone once observed.

And on the wall of Price's cubicle at the city detective bureau was a single page, framed in black, with the signal Nelson sent to his fleet before the battle at Trafalgar. "England expects that every man will do his duty," it read.

"What the hell does that mean?" one of Price's colleagues inquired when he noticed the statement for the first time.

"It means you ought to get your ragged ass out of here and solve a crime," he replied without looking up from the file that engaged his attention. He had barely noticed that the inquiry came from Michael James Francis Dunston, chief of detectives and his immediate boss. The two were friends and had been rookies together many years earlier, but Dunston, an able, affable and largely straight-forward man, could employ diplomacy in his dealings with the police hierarchy when necessary. Price was entirely devoid of that ability, which accounted for the difference in their departmental ranks. As far as Price was concerned, that difference was moot. He had no ambition to advance beyond his present station, detective first class, because he knew that further advancement led only to expanded administrative responsibilities and political entanglements.

"I reviewed your report on this Barnes character," Dunston said, "and I think it's time to close the file. There's not enough evidence to bring charges and he's not only out of our jurisdiction, he's probably on another planet by now."

Price pushed his file aside, looked up and nodded agreement. "I know," he said with absolutely no intention of dropping the matter. He had recognized some time earlier that the pursuit of Toby Barnes was no longer a departmental concern, but he had been unable to separate himself from the case.

"Do you?" Dunston asked, knowing Price as well as anyone and reasonably certain his response had been uncharacteristically agreeable. He knew his long-time friend had great difficulty separating himself from unsolved cases and he thought this one would be no exception.

"I understand the department has probably done as much as it can," Price said, "but there's no reason I can't spend a little of my own time on this thing. I know more about Toby Barnes from this investigation than anybody ought to know about anybody else, but there are still too many loose ends . . . too many things I don't know."

"That's not always a bad thing," Dunston replied. "You know what I've always said about ignorance. It may not be bliss, but it does have a certain soothing effect." Knowing Price as he did, he had no doubt their conversation was little more than idle chatter and that his friend would pursue the matter until he either resolved the case or it was absolutely clear the issue was beyond remedy. And the chief of detectives was right, as usual.

Price was a competent fresh water sailor, a recreational past-time that had developed from his interest in history and the widely held human desire to congregate near large bodies of moisture. He owned an old 19-foot class boat he kept and sailed on Lake Millstone, a vast impoundment less than 50 miles from the city. Created when one of the state's secondary rivers was dammed to create hydroelectric power for the region, the lake had broad reaches of open water and steady wind, unimpeded by a largely barren shoreline mostly owned by the utility that generated the electric power.

In his spare time during the moderate seasons, Price often sailed his boat and worked on it much as he worked on the model of Nelson's flagship. He did it more for therapy and an opportunity to think than to complete the task, and both boats - one a model and the other an actual sailing vessel - were soon employed as devices in his thoughtful search for ways to pursue Toby Barnes. He hoped Barnes had remained in the Caribbean, not so much because it was more convenient than most of the likely options but because it would provide him an opportunity and excuse to sail for the first time in salt water.

Price's principal sailing partner was Jack McCurdy, another old friend who had once been a city detective but now practiced the same occupation in a near-by suburb where he lived with his wife, Missy, and their five children. McCurdy had worked with him in an unofficial way during the early stages of the Barnes case, but had mainly through inadvertence or, as Price told him, sheer blind luck gotten physically involved with two women, both central to the case, at the same time. Not experienced in that kind of behavior, his deception was soon discovered by his wife, who threw him out of their house for a time and then reconciled with her regretful husband under terms that greatly reduced his prior freedom. He was still allowed to sail with Price, but he was off the case.

Actually, McCurdy was only off the case as far as his wife and the two other women were concerned. He meant to keep his promise of future fidelity to his wife but had no intention of leaving the Barnes investigation to Price alone. Although he had absolutely no official capacity in the case and had only gotten involved in the first place as a favor to his old friend, he shared with Price the bloodhound instinct that kept him on a trail that was all but cold. McCurdy told Price he would assist in any way he could short of revealing that assistance to his wife, whose level of suspicion was constant and considerable.

Price, who knew his resources were ridiculously insufficient compared with those of Toby Barnes, counted himself lucky to have even the limited help of McCurdy, an investigator of proven ability, and he also knew he could secure occasional support from Mike Dunston. Throughout his professional career, the chief of detectives had developed ties with law enforcement officials and others in related fields around the globe and, if pressed by Price, would on very rare occasions employ these contacts for him. Price understood that Dunston could not officially sanction further investigation in the case but, given his trans-oceanic reach, might well enable him to regain the lost trail.

Dunston was inclined to give Price more latitude than anyone else in the department, but it was never an issue with anyone because he granted it so sparingly. Most of the other detectives, if they noticed at all, assumed the two were simply old friends, but there was a good deal more to it than an ancient chumminess. Price, early in their poice careers, had saved Dunston's life.

As rookie uniformed patrolmen, the two had been partnered one snowy night when an outbreak of flu temporarily depleted the ranks and forced a change in normal department policy that paired newcomers with experienced officers. They were cruising in an old, crime-ridden neighborhood when, almost simultaneously, they received a radio alert to a convenience store robbery and saw the apparent robber depart the premises, gun in hand. He dashed toward a nearby car, which they managed to block with their police cruiser, and the felon then changed course into the nearest alley. Dunston, who was in the passenger seat of the cruiser, was out the door and after him with Price not far behind. All three raced full tilt, unaware the alleyway was covered with a sheet of ice until Dunston hit a particularly treacherous patch and lost his footing. He slid heavily into a brick wall and was knocked flat on his back, where he lay stunned as the robber turned, saw his advantage and leveled his gun at the young police officer. Price, who saw Dunston fall, had instinctively drawn his .38 police special when he realized the assumed felon was prepared to shoot his partner. The alley was dark but a single security light over a loading dock provided just enough illumination for Price to see and hit his target with a clean shot through the chest. Dunston later marveled at the marksmanship, which Price attributed to "plain dumb luck."

Price was not one to call in old debts for his personal benefit, but he was not above using his leverage with Dunston to do departmental work. And even though the department had essentially signed off on the Barnes case, it remained active as far as Price was concerned. He was a man whose sense of justice sometimes paralleled the system and sometimes went in contrary directions.

In his late 40s, Price retained the natural strength he inherited from unknown ancestors and over the years supplemented those endowments with weight and martial arts training. He disliked the effort, which he considered boring, but he knew there were a raft of bad people who had grown incredibly strong in prison weight lifting areas. He knew prison officials used weight lifting to let inmates work off excess energy that might otherwise be directed to mischief in one form or another, but he questioned the prudence of creating a society of very strong criminals. Price knew he couldn't change the system, so he did his best to prepare for whatever situation might confront him in a dangerous business.

McCurdy was no weakling, but he had little appetite for physical exercise other than an occasional golf game or batting soft balls in the park to his young sons. Naturally good natured, he only fought, even as a youngster, when pushed to his limits, although his enormous adult hands were useful in controlling the occasional prisoner or as imposing fists on those rare occasions when they were needed for one purpose or another. He was somewhat shorter and bulkier than Price, but the two often dressed like a matched set, inexpensive dark blue suits, white shirts, striped ties and polished black shoes. They looked like the cops they were, and were not surprised when strangers instantly identified their occupations.

Price hadn't saved McCurdy's life, but he did save his friend's house. Not much of a financial manager, Jack McCurdy had been strapped for money even before he and his wife, Missy, accumulated their five children. The growth of their family substantially outpaced the rise in his salary and that simple arithmetic fact combined with sheer fiscal incompetence brought him to the brink of mortgage foreclosure. Price learned of the situation by accident and used his own money – more than $20,00 – to restore the mortgage to financial health, all without McCurdy's initial knowledge. McCurdy, in fact, was embarrassed and incensed when he discovered his friend's gesture, and only accepted the money to keep his wife and children off the streets. "You miserable, goddamn capitalist," he said to Price at the time, "why don't you mind your own fucking business."

"You are my business," Price replied calmly, "although I have to admit you're a pretty poor excuse for an enterprise of any kind."

McCurdy took the money and paid it back over a five-year period, learning in that time something about prudence and austerity. He had wanted to add a reasonable interest charge to what he considered a loan and Price had originally meant as a gift, but Price refused that money with the explanation he was a policeman and not a banker. Once past his initial embarrassment and long before he had repaid the debt, McCurdy realized the extent of their friendship. He knew Price had moderate resources but the amount of his generosity was significant in that time before his aunt's estate increased his financial independence. The two men never discussed the matter, even as McCurdy systematically mailed checks to Price until he had discharged the debt with those payments and a final $10,000 installment made possible by an inheritance Missy McCurdy received on the death of a distant relative.

The loan to McCurdy was surely a gesture of friendship, but the two men established their real bond at Lake Millstone where they usually sailed alone or, occasionally, were joined by Missy McCurdy or, even more rarely, a couple of the McCurdy children. Neither the boat nor Price's patience could accommodate all seven of the McCurdys at the same time.

Price and McCurdy not only enjoyed sailing but liked the maintenance work as well, particularly in the early spring when they brought the boat out of its winter storage or in the late fall when stiff breezes across the open water forecast the coming winter. They sailed or worked, but always discussed various crimes under investigation in their separate police departments until their alliance on the Barnes case made it a single issue in most of their conversations.

"I think," Price said early one sunny afternoon as he skippered the boat and they sailed a long reach on Lake Millstone, "that Barnes is set on buying or building another ranch, somewhere in some remote place where he's not likely to be bothered with the past."

"Maybe," McCurdy replied, tightening one of the lines, "but that could be almost anywhere in the frigging world."

"You're right in one respect," Price agreed, "but not in another. He has the money to go almost anywhere he wants to go, but he also wants, I'm willing to bet, a big spread in an out-of-the-way place. He not only wants a big spread, he wants a first class operation, and those requirements will greatly limit his possibilities."

"Yeah," McCurdy said after a moment's reflection, "that means we're only looking for a bigger needle in the haystack."

Price conceded the search wouldn't be easy, but pointed out the combination of Dunston's far-flung police connections and the proliferation of electronic records made it at least possible. "Someone, somewhere might surely notice an operation on the scale that Barnes would undertake," he suggested, "and alerting every cop from here to the last hamlet and village in the world is entirely possible, assuming Dunston is agreeable to the idea."

Price thought it might also be useful to monitor the activities of a local lawyer who had the ambiguous distinction of representing a small-time local mobster, Albert Moretti, and Toby Barnes. The ambiguity derived from the near certainty that Barnes had shot Moretti to death in the belief the man had, with an accomplice, murdered his father many years earlier. The attorney, Sonny Spivak, had represented Moretti and other felonious types for a long time, but Barnes had only engaged him recently to handle certain matters with cloudy ethical implications. Price suspected Spivak had alerted Toby Barnes in the British Virgin Islands that his presence there had been detected, and that the police were about to appear on his doorstep. Spivak apparently used private investigators to get the information, which gave Barnes the chance to disappear only a day ahead of Price's arrival in the tropics.

The boat – which Price had named Graf Spee after the pocket battle ship the Germans scuttled during the second world war to prevent its capture by the British – was secure in its rented slip and the two sailors had found barstools in The Lake Millstone Boat & Tennis Club, which had no tennis courts and had been named by its founders to prove they had senses of humor. Opened only on weekends, the club sold hot dogs, chips, beef jerky and several brands of domestic beer.

"This place could use a fresh coat of paint," Diana Hornbeck, Price's friend and a good deal more, observed as she joined them at the bar from a small table where she had been doing weekend paperwork while they sailed the Graf Spee.

"That," Price replied, "would greatly diminish its charm and I, for one, would resign my membership."

Diana, who had only known Price for a matter of months, had not been to the lake before and had only agreed to make the trip if she were left alone for a while to complete urgent work for the advertising agency that employed her as one of its vice presidents. "I'm serious," she insisted. "Surely the members of this goat farm could scrape together enough money for a few cans of stark white paint. There are state penitentiaries that aren't as dingy as this place." She put her slender business case full of papers on the bar and gracefully ascended a stool as Price captured the volunteer bartender's attention and ordered a beer for her.

"And," she added, "they might stock a decent German beer instead of this domestic swill that's only acceptable at ball parks and the occasional company picnic."

Price smiled approvingly, barely conscious of the reality that Diana's flippant manner had attracted him almost as much as her good looks and passionate nature. He had, however, come to understand that her commentaries, meant usually in fun, were only surface expressions of real intelligence. He had gradually begun to confide in her things he would never have revealed to anyone outside the department. She knew more about the Barnes case than anyone with the exception of Jack McCurdy, and she had this information because Price had come to value her judgment.

"Jack," Diana said, addressing McCurdy, "what did you two sleuths decide out there on the open water?"

"Not much, but it sure was a nice day."

Price was about to recount his earlier discussion with McCurdy for Diana when he was interrupted by the tinkling sound of the cell phone he had meant to turn off. The instrument played "Mary Had A Little Lamb" in his jacket pocket for the moments before he was able to find and answer it. "Yeah," he said into the mouthpiece with little regard for telephone conventions. And "yeah" he repeated several times at intervals until, finally and after a few minutes, he concluded the conversation with a curt "Thanks."

"You are an articulate man," Diana observed, effectively disguising her genuine curiosity about the call in much the same way she disguised her genuine affection for Price.

"That was Dunston," Price revealed. "He just got word from a contact in South America that Barnes may be dead."

McCurdy took a prolonged, thoughtful sip from his frosty beer bottle. "Do you believe it?" he asked Price.

"We'll see," was the response.

*

Chapter Three

Diana Hornbeck's father, John, had been a career diplomat whose lack of personal diplomacy had relegated him and, consequently, his family to a long series of postings in remote and occasionally dangerous places. He was a man of considerable intelligence and conscience with an inability to keep his vision of the whole truth to himself. This quirk of nature was an impediment to his career, but the extensive travel it sponsored gave Diana, who had inherited his intellectual smartness along with a certain practical outlook that eluded her father, with a broad experience of the world that eventually made her a rather sophisticated adult.

Diana was an only child whose precocity was indulged by two loving parents who failed to realize her transient life was an extended and invaluable education and not the hindrance they assumed it was. Her mother, Christine or Crissy, had grown up in the American south as part of a large conventional family and thought her daughter had been deprived of the sheltering environment needed to produce a socially adjusted adult. Unaware as a child of her parents concerns, she simply enjoyed the concessions she derived from their feelings of guilt until, in her mid-teens, she was kidnapped by a small band of insurgents in the shaky Central American dictatorship where her father served at the time. Or, that was the story she told her parents and the authorities when she emerged from a tropical jungle several weeks later.

Actually, Diana had met a young man – also a teenager but one two years her senior – in the market square, and had willingly accompanied him into the jungle where he was part of a rag-tag band of desperate men who fought, when they were able, a corrupt and mainly incompetent government military force. Her attraction to the young man was purely hormonal and had nothing to do with local political notions. She had originally intended to have a single, deflowering episode with him, but the intensity of their first experience together led to an affair that lasted for weeks. Physically strong and graced with natural athletic aptitude, Diana was able to keep up with the band, which was constantly on the move through dense rain forests and over rugged, low mountain trails to avoid detection and confrontation with their enemies. Her Spanish – which was the country's national language – was fluent and she made no demands on the group, who were not kidnappers and were perfectly willing to let her go free had that been her wish.

The young man, Diego, had less than a year earlier fled to the jungle to evade military justice. He had killed a soldier who had raped and murdered his sister, he told Diana, but he didn't tell her he had slit the man's throat, surgically removed his penis and left that organ in the victim's mouth to advertise his revenge. The act, quite naturally, had antagonized the authorities, and they had unsuccessfully pursued him through a jungle he had known since childhood. Their pursuit and his evasions taught the young man a great deal about survival, and eventually brought him into contact with the small group of rebels who instructed him in the use of the various firearms mostly acquired from soldiers they had killed in various ambushes and other guerilla activities.

Motivated mainly by simple lust and a genuine attraction to her young lover, Diana had been unaware of the real danger in her situation until the band accidentally stumbled across a government patrol one day and found itself in a firefight with a heavily armed opponent. The density of the jungle combined with her youthful agility and simple good luck enabled her to slip away unnoticed, but she would remember throughout her life the sound of military ammunition peppering the heavy growth above her head as she slithered from the battleground.

She crawled for a considerable distance, finally putting the sound of gunshots behind her and blundering onto a trail that for all she knew could have been made by large forest beasts. The trail, it turned out, led to a small village of indigenous people who saw this scratched, bruised and lightly bloodied young woman and took immediate pity on her. They applied herbal remedies to superficial wounds, fed and returned her to the authorities, who were still and would remain under the assumption she had been kidnapped. Diana, even as a young woman, disliked liars and lying, but she also understood that truth, under certain circumstances, did little good for anyone and could actually have quite the opposite effect. For that reason mostly and also because she rather enjoyed the fiction, she went along with the kidnapping story to ease both her parents concerns, once they knew she was safe, and those of the authorities who relied heavily on U.S. military assistance and other forms of charity.

The one sad element in her little adventure was the belief Diego had surely been killed in the skirmish with government troops. She had, quite naturally, never before experienced a jungle firefight and the sounds of flying bullets and battle cries gave her the impression the engagement was far deadlier than the reality. There was a good deal of shooting and yelling, but there were actually no casualties on either side. The insurgents, among them Diego, escaped into the dense forest and he, like her, thought the other had died in the conflict. But life went on for both of them.

Diana's parents, who had suffered far more than she had during the alleged ordeal, were enormously relieved to regain their daughter and to learn her virtue had been miraculously preserved. She told them and the authorities there had been no rape or mistreatment, probably because the band was constantly on the move and had little time for those collateral activities. She provided a good deal of misinformation to protect herself and also to provide what assistance she could to the rebels, who she had come to admire during her short alliance with them. The episode, however, was one John and Crissy Hornbeck were not willing to repeat and they soon made arrangements to send Diana to a respectable New England boarding school under the assumption that was a safer environment than a small Central American dictatorship in the throes of a mostly unsuccessful insurrection. Diana was less than thrilled by this prospect but had little power to prevent an action that would transport her from a warm, colorful place where she had almost absolute freedom to the drab coldness of a northern educational institution founded on the notion that rigidity and conformity were somehow virtuous. She was at the time only vaguely aware she had closely brushed death and totally oblivious to her great good luck in avoiding pregnancy, a condition that would have complicated her life far more than the transfer from the tropics to what she later described as "The Tundra." Somewhat later when the facts of life had penetrated her youthful consciousness, she realized the extent of her luck. But that was later.

She was trundled off to the Maidenhead School for Girls by parents who would desperately miss her, but saw their duty and did it. Knowing what she did about her recent adventure but unable to confide the real facts to anyone, Diana learned something about the ambiguity of successful lies. She eventually came to the conclusion her duplicity had been for the best, although it had altered her life in a way she had neither foreseen nor appreciated. The lie had done its work, but the result was less than perfect.

As Diana pursued an entirely new life in New England, the young guerilla, Diego Martinez, was pursued in an entirely different manner through jungles, fields and villages as well as over and around mountains and hills by a succession of military units, some small and others larger but all equally unsuccessful. The rebels would occasionally turn on their pursuers in ambush, usually to replenish their arms and supplies, but were always prudent in recognition of their essential weakness in terms of both personnel and resources. They did relatively little physical damage to their enemy, but were a considerable psychological problem to a government that seemed unable to defeat them. They were only "a gnat on an elephant's ass," Diego told Toby Barnes many years later when they had become close friends, but neither the government nor the general public –

particularly the poor farmers who worked the interior lands – understood their essential weakness. They eventually gained a reputation for fearless aggression that was neither their purpose nor capacity, and became part of a rural mythology that made heroes of a scraggly band of men who were mostly trying to survive in an almost impossible situation.

Diego -- whose murder of the government soldier gave him little choice – remained with the insurgents, learning a deadly trade that enabled him not only to survive, but to eventually assume a leadership position within the group. He was smart, cunning, physically strong and seemingly fearless, which meant he was able to conceal his fear in situations he knew were dangerous. "Only a fool is without fear when it's justified," he later told Barnes, implying the real trick is to perform effectively despite those fears.

The lives of these two men – Diego Martinez and Toby Barnes – were to intersect in a jungle region that was as unlikely as it was remote. Martinez had by that time matured into the unquestioned leader of his group, and Barnes was a veteran Special Forces sergeant who had conducted secret missions in even more remote parts of the globe. This one was meant to clandestinely interdict an enormous drug shipment destined for the United States and to destroy both the drugs and the well-armed thugs who meant to carry out this substantial enterprise. Barnes and his handful of tough specialists could only succeed if the element of surprise was on their side, and that was only possible if their force was small and took up ambush positions along a narrow jungle trail without alerting their quarry. The plan had been devised by U.S. government agents who naively confided the information to a corrupt local police official who, in turn, passed it along to his confederates in the drug trade. As a consequence, Barnes and his men were ambushed and certainly would have died in that steamy backwater had it not been for their superior tactical skills and the accidental intervention of Diego's rebels, who hated the drug people as much as they hated their government. The hired thugs who worked for the drug lord had the advantage of surprise, but had not picked the best place along the trail for their attack. They were men accustomed to guns employed for murder at very close range, but they were not tactical fighters and one of them commenced firing before Barnes and his men were securely trapped. The Special Forces unit quickly backed off the trail, took up a strong defensive position but were never-the-less in a precarious situation. They were pinned down in a damp, smelly, bug-infested, light-starved tropical forest and their prospects were bleak at best. These men, however, were mostly optimists, despite strong cynical inclinations, or they wouldn't have chosen the work that had brought them to their predicament. Given that general disposition, most of them were only mildly surprised when after several hours of stalemate they realized their attackers were themselves under attack.

There was little in that part of the jungle that eluded Diego's attention, and he had learned from indigenous sources that members of the drug organization had for some unusual reason taken up hidden positions along a principal trail. He didn't know who they intended to ambush but assumed that their enemy must surely be his friend, an assumption that in the long run was as close to prophesy as any mortal is likely to get.

Diego's men infiltrated the dense brush behind the ambushers and opened a withering volley of gunfire that forced their targets to flee directly into an even more devastating hail from the automatic weapons employed by Barnes and his unit. In less than 15 minutes the skirmish was over, and more than two dozen thugs lay either dead or dying on the narrow trail. The two surviving sides cautiously identified themselves to one another across the body-strewn and blood-splattered pathway before they emerged from their separate covers. At the time, Diego spoke little English but Barnes knew enough Spanish to explain the situation and express gratitude for an action that had probably saved his life and those of his men. He also noted the ragged condition of the guerillas and told them he would try but could not promise to ease their situation with money, supplies and anything else he might extract from the bungling planners who had put him and his men in harm's way. Given Diego's long war with the U.S.-backed government, he also explained, the task would not be an easy one. But he assured the rebel leader they would meet again, and that was a promise he was able to keep.

Barnes, who had fought many bitter campaigns in unpublicized, out-of-the-way places where his death would have gone unnoticed and unappreciated, knew he had pressed his luck beyond any reasonable point. Knowing that and no longer interested in military life, he had decided to muster out of the army and find an occupation with more extended prospects. The debacle in the jungle reinforced that notion, and also provided inspiration for a plan that would make a more tolerable life possible for him.

Barnes knew from sources he had cultivated on several continents and elsewhere that an international drug lord based his operations in a fortress-like mansion built on a small, rocky mountain that rose out of the very jungle where Diego and his men had lived precariously for years. He also knew from these sources that drug revenues were not only laundered and stashed in various off-shore and other mainly unsupervised banking institutions, but that great sums of this money had been translated into precious metals and stones that were in all probability stored in the drug lord's jungle bastion. And he had learned on his own that the killers who made this enterprise possible were an undisciplined rabble that might be effectively overwhelmed by a smaller, well-trained force. Knowing and suspecting all this, Barnes decided to leave the army and conduct one final mission that would make him a wealthy man and at the same time settle his score with the drug lord.

Once discharged from military service, the former sergeant methodically recruited a small group of former Special Forces soldiers and similar types with proven combat credentials and also enlisted Diego Martinez and several of his most trusted men for an assault on the very center of this worldwide drug enterprise. He financed his project with more than $200,000 accumulated from the sale of contraband diamonds acquired along with information about the Central American drug business from a captured rebel leader who had operated on the borders of several African countries. He had traded diamonds stolen from mines and individuals in his part of the world for drugs – which were usually more marketable than the diamonds – from anywhere. Barnes had captured this man in an earlier clandestine assignment and allowed him to barter his life for the money and information. At the same time, Barnes had bartered his integrity and would gamble his life for a chance to start over.

Diego Martinez, too, realized he had cheated the odds too many times in his continuing engagements with local army units and the police, and was more than willing to join Barnes in a final effort to evade the early death that otherwise seemed inevitable. He was also attracted to the generous up-front cash payments made to all the men with the understanding far more would be forthcoming if the venture was a success. Barnes, however, made it clear to the group he would claim the lion's share and there would be no renegotiation of their agreements. In addition to his life, he gambled more than $200,000 in an effort to gain what he considered real wealth.

The drug lord – a man known only as Zee – had operated from his jungle stronghold for more than a decade, but little was known of his origins or the exact nature of his vast and often deadly enterprises. A man of medium height, he was large-boned and beefy with a bull neck that suggested he had once been an enforcer of some kind, although his extraordinary success in an incredibly tough business revealed a very cunning, if not intelligent, nature. He had unusually light skin, inherited, perhaps, from the Spaniards who had conquered the regions that carried on their linguistic tradition, but broad features that were more like the Indians whose lives and cultures they plundered.

Zee was a man whose implacability was based on a cruel streak that was central to his nature. He used cruelty to achieve practical goals, but he also seemed to enjoy its application. He was known to have killed people on whims, sometimes on the premises of his fortress home. The structure, originally much smaller, had been the residence of a successful planter, who had built it atop the small mountain for its view of the surrounding jungle and to protect himself from the natives he exploited and who occasionally rose up in protest against his type. There had once been a trail leading to the outside world, but Zee had allowed tropical growth to obliterate that access and now relied on a helicopter to ferry him away and back to the place. The pad where it took off and landed was on top of the entire structure, which had been expanded over the years with stone from the mountainside. From a distance, it looked like an ancient Mayan construction, lacking only the near vertical stairways of the old temples. Inside, however, the various spaces had only bad taste in common. Zee had lavished his great wealth on every extravagance that could be transported, sometimes in sections or pieces, into the complex by air. There were large hot tubs, pink-cushioned pool tables, outlandishly ornate and varied furniture, vast expanses of velvet drapery and deep-pile carpeting in colors rarely compatible with anything else.

There were also young women, flown in and out for drunken parties that Zee and his lieutenants devised to occupy the tropical nights, and these debaucheries sometimes resulted in rape, other brutalities and, occasionally, murder. Two of the rape victims were to provide Barnes with detailed information on the interior layout of Zee's stronghold, intelligence that would have been otherwise difficult to discover. Almost girls, the young women had been lured to the mountain from a distant village by one of the drug lord's agents, who told them only they would have a good time and that their host was a generous man. They were neither virgins nor unaware of the sexual implications in the invitation, but they had not anticipated the rough vulgarity of the men they met nor the multiple rapes they endured before the evening was over and they were dispatched by helicopter away from the dreadful place. Their stories came to Diego, who had grown up in their village and retained strong ties to his ancestral home. He subsequently passed the information along to Barnes, who immediately recognized its value.

One of the young women, Maria, was both beautiful and intelligent, qualities that accounted for both her invitation to Zee's stronghold and for her ability to provide Diego with a great deal of detailed information about its general layout. She had been dragged from bedroom to bedroom, screaming epithets at her abusers, and on several occasions had been able to escape down a hallway or stairway before she was recaptured and hauled off to the nearest horizontal surface. Luckily for her, this defiance seemed to amuse and arouse her defilers, who otherwise might have killed her for the inconvenience she caused them. Instead, they gave the women $1,000 each when - bruised, trembling and exhausted - they were finally dumped unceremoniously onto the helicopter and flown away.

Among the men who had Maria that night was Zee, whose preeminence was apparent in the way the others deferred to him, and whose bedroom was singular for its size and appointments. She was able to describe him in extraordinary detail to Diego, recalling everything from the heavy scent of an expensive cologne he wore to the inadequate size of his penis. "That pig," she said in reference to him on a number of occasions, aware he was the one centrally responsible for her ordeal. Fortunately for her, Diego realized, she had not confided her opinion of his organ to Zee.

Diego listened to everything she said and was able to mentally reconstruct the stronghold interior down to the color of drapes and carpet in some rooms. Maria recalled these details and many others with harsh contempt for the place as well as those who had misused her. As he listened to her story, he also noticed, despite the fading facial bruises, her beauty as well as her courage and resilience. Sometime before his interview with her concluded, Diego had fallen in love but it was a condition he would not fully recognize until later.

Early on the last day of Zee's life when the sun had not yet risen and the tropical birds still slept, Barnes and his men commenced their assault on the stronghold. Inside, the drug lord and most of his men had only retired a few hours earlier and even the sentries who manned strategic parapets were listless from their long, lonely vigils. These defenders were the first to die, victims of the hard men who had scaled the mountain, unseen, and shot them at relatively short range, and the meticulous plan Barnes devised based on information gathered by spotters Diego had assigned to the area. Once onto the building, the attackers quickly found the hallways and descended into the interior just as Zee's men, most of them half asleep and half dressed, appeared from various rooms and fell before barrages of automatic gunfire. The deep morning silence had been broken not only by the sound of gunfire, but also by occasional explosions from hand grenades tossed into certain areas to achieve tactical results.

Zee – whose vast bedroom was deep in the central structure – slept soundly through the initial stages of the attack and was only awakened when Diego kicked his expensive door down and appeared like a bad dream. The drug lord fumbled desperately for the .45 on the nightstand next to his bed, but a concentrated round of fire from Diego's automatic weapon obliterated the stand and shredded what had been Zee's right arm. But he was still alive when Diego put a strong hand under his chin, forced it back and with a very large knife slit his throat so thoroughly his head would have fallen off his body had it not been on a pillow. His eyes, sleepy only moments earlier, bulged with the instantaneous but fatal realization.

The treasure Barnes sought proved even more lavish than he had expected, providing not only a considerable fortune in gems and precious metals but detailed off-shore bank records that eventually enabled him to recover many millions more in various currencies. This treasure and the records were found in a single storeroom deep within the fortress, and its contents, carefully itemized and put into backpacks, was carried off the mountain by Barnes and his men, who as they left set off strategically placed explosive charges that demolished the structure beyond future use. The bodies of Zee and his thugs were interred under a massive pile of debris that, as it settled, became an organic part of the mountain.

Barnes, now wealthy beyond even his original expectations, settled generously with his men, who scattered in various directions as their leader went on to assume a series of identities meant to secure his privacy. He appeared in the Ozarks, where he established a large ranch and a reputation to match, as Jake Pritchard, and later in the British Virgin Islands, where he had gone as Paul Striker with his companion, Isabella, to evade Bill Price and anyone else with an interest in his affairs. He decamped the tropics just ahead of Price, who assumed he had taken on still another identity.

Diego Martinez, meanwhile, had allied himself permanently with both Barnes and Maria, whose physical and other qualities soon induced him to marry her. The couple adapted quickly to the Ozark ranch project, where Diego proved he could manage livestock as well as men, and Maria's convent education, which included English learned from American nuns, enabled her to handle various responsibilities and to teach her new husband a second language.

Diana Hornbeck had not seen Diego since their separation as

teenagers and assumed he had died in that humid jungle many years earlier. She had been shipped off to North America for schooling and an eventual career in advertising, which engaged her attention until a night in a place called The Bristol Bar and Grill where she met Bill Price and they commenced a relationship based on mutual affection and simple lust. She would accompany Price to the Ozarks when he sought to confront Toby Barnes on his ranch, and was unaware she had missed by only days an opportunity to meet again the man, Diego, who had captured her girlhood virginity. Their failure to meet was probably just as well, given the certainty that fictional coincidence seems far less probable than the same thing in reality.

*

Chapter Four

The pilot – a man whose robust size drew the attention of several Chilean airport officials – had filed a flight plan that originated in Santiago and terminated at Buenos Aires in Argentina, a reasonably long haul for the turbo-prop aircraft but one well within its 1200 mile range. The failure of the plane to reach its destination might have gone unnoticed amid the general volume of commercial and private air traffic around these two large population centers had not Mike Dunston issued an alert to specific South and Central American police contacts based on information supplied by Bill Price.

The plane had gone missing and the Latin American authorities assumed it had crashed, probably somewhere along its flight path in Argentina. Given the lack of any communication from the aircraft, there was the further assumption the pilot and three passengers had died in a routine aviation accident even though no sign of wreckage had yet or was ever discovered. The news of the alleged accident combined with descriptions of the pilot and his passengers were the basis for the Barnes death report sent to Dunston and relayed to Price at the Millstone Boat and Tennis Club.

But Price soon realized the report was inconclusive and that the slippery Barnes had probably negotiated another one of his tricky deceptions. The plane, he noted, was similar to the one Barnes had flown from the continental U.S. to the American Virgin Islands, a fast turbo-prop with near very light jet performance but an aircraft that could land on a dirt strip less than 3,000 feet long. That meant Barnes could and, Price concluded, probably had some rural Argentine destination rather than the one designated in his flight plan.

The description of the pilot and three passengers left little doubt that Barnes, Isabella, Diego and Maria were aboard the plane, which turned out to be the same Beechcraft Kingair the fugitive had flown from the States to St. Thomas in the Virgin Islands. He had left it there when he and Isabella crossed by boat to the British Virgins to elude pursuit, and apparently arranged later for someone to clandestinely fly the equipment, presumably in stages, to South America. Barnes could easily have written the plane off and purchased something else, but his nature, Price was beginning to suspect, was too frugal for that kind of waste. There was some truth to that suspicion, but there was the reality that Barnes had hidden several million dollars in currency aboard the plane and simply wanted to retrieve the money. And once he had done that, there was no reason, in his estimation, not to use the equipment.

The information sent to Dunston was premature in its report or even suggestion the plane had crashed and Barnes had not survived, but it did provide an insight into his general location and the new name he had used to cloak his true identity. The pilot, according to the Latin American authorities, was Milos Cherbic, and the three passengers had been equipped with equally false, although Latin-sounding, surnames. But his size, traveling companions, aircraft preference as well as other unique characteristics were hard to disguise and produced the first lead in what until then had been a stalled case.

Barnes had transformed himself to Jake Pritchard, Paul Striker and, now, to Milos Cherbic, an interesting ethnic diversion, Price thought, wondering at the time what had inspired the latest choice. And had he combined the new name with a phony European accent of some variety or was he content to remain an American? Price soon concluded the answers made no difference since Barnes would surely invent still another identity before long.

"Barnes is a considerable mystery in one respect, but he's as transparent as window glass in another," Price had told his friend and boss, chief of detectives Mike Dunston. "The time, effort and money he put into that Ozark ranch tells me it was done to satisfy some basic urge and not simply as an investment." Price had learned a good deal about the ranch from Sheriff Jones in Stockton. The locals had called the place "over-improved," meaning simply that Barnes had spent well beyond the practical needs of the operation. He had spent many thousands of dollars that were not likely to be recovered in any practical way, which informed Price the project had deep personal significance for its owner.

"He's got a lot of money and he knows the wide world," Price had also told Dunston, who had ordered him to officially close out the murder investigation, but had also inferred he would not interfere if it were carried on in an extra-curricular manner. "I think he's likely to build or buy another ranch in some remote but stable part of the world . . . some place where large parcels of land are available and where there are no wars, revolutions or other forms of hostility." Price assumed Barnes had mustered out of the army to put conflicts of that nature behind him, an assumption based on simple common sense. Those who have witnessed warfare first hand generally have a preference for more peaceful environments, particularly if they intend to run permanent, productive enterprises.

"I'm inclined to suspect he'll wind up somewhere in Latin America, mainly because he's reasonably fluent in Spanish and seems to like the Latin cultures," Price continued. "He also has a side-kick from somewhere south of our border who he treats more like a friend than a subordinate." The reference was to Diego Martinez whose precise nationality had never been determined by those who met him in the Stockton area but whose heavy accent at the time clearly identified his native language as Spanish. Most of the people who met him in the Ozarks simply assumed he was from Mexico.

Diego steadily improved his English with tutelage from Maria as well as daily use of the language, and his general manner, formerly rough from the hard scrabble life he had lived as a youngster and later as a hunted rebel, smoothed rapidly under the influence of Barnes and Isabella. They essentially taught him the rules of a more prosperous society and refined the man down to his selection of clothes and basic hygiene, which had not concerned him much in the Central American jungle. Maria, too, was influenced in much the same way, although she was initially far more refined than Diego.

Barnes probably owed his life to Diego, but there was more to the bond of friendship that developed between them. Despite the great differences in their cultural origins and appearance, there were many similarities in their fundamental personalities. Barnes was the ultimate gringo with skin that would have been pale had he not spent so much time out-of-doors. He had a broad, friendly face when he wanted it to appear that way and close cut, sand-colored hair tinged with pre-mature gray. He was more than six feet four in height, but his broad chest and massive shoulders made him appear much larger. In contrast, Diego's black hair, brown skin and high cheekbones suggested a dark prince, someone who had seen things others were not meant to see. He, too, gave the impression of strength, although his height was no more than five ten.

Side by side, they were a study in contrasts, but their interiors were quite similar in many ways. They were both capable of murder as well as gentleness, and they conducted their lives under a simple code of honor that required no written or oral expression, only an intuitive knowledge of its requirements. They were both intelligent, practical and adaptable to changing circumstances and each of them recognized these qualities in the other.

As far as Barnes was concerned, Price knew his man, at least in the broad sweep of his character and ambitions. He had learned about him in the course of an intense investigation that revealed much about his formative years, although very little about the military career that had forged the finished personality. But there were useful fragments – his time in the Ozarks, for one – that shed some light on the adult Barnes and with everything else gave Price the basis for his insights. He had predicted Barnes would reappear somewhere in Latin America, a generalization, he realized, that covered a lot of ground.

At the time, however, Price did not realize the full accuracy of his assessment. He had not only predicted the man's geographical intentions, but his principal purpose as well. Barnes had gone to the

Argentine to inspect a large tract of land in the Pampas, a vast monotonous grassland that extends from the Atlantic Ocean to the Andean foothills. There are ranches throughout the Pampas, where cattle have grazed since their introduction by the Portuguese in the 1550s. By the 18th century, there were wild herds that roamed the region, hunted by the famous gauchos or Argentine cowboys for their skins and fat. Many of the original gauchos were of mixed Spanish and black descent who had crossed the border from Brazil to escape slavery. But that was an historical matter of little concern to Barnes, whose single-minded interest at the time was limited to the acquisition of land.

Barnes and his party flew directly to a large estancia or ranch owned by an elderly man whose ancestors had settled the land before the gauchos were relegated to romantic history and large agricultural enterprises began the ruin of a grasslands ecosystem that had evolved over many thousands of years. The owner, Oscar Medina -- tall and stately with a thinning white mustache -- met the visitors at his private airstrip, not far from the large, rambling structure that had been his home for more than 80 years. He was the sole survivor of a family that had died out through a series of accidents and illnesses that would have destroyed a lesser person, but the accumulated tragedies in his life had left his ancient face furrowed with lines and his eyes saddened beyond expression. He sought a buyer for the ranch who would maintain its traditional cattle business and resist the profitable temptation to turn its fertile soil to crop production. He hated farmers with the reinforced animosities of many years, but he kept those feelings to himself.

"Mr. Cherbic, I gather," he greeted Barnes and the others as they left the plane. Medina's English was crisp and fluent, learned as a boy and cultivated through many trips to the British Isles and North America. He had also traveled widely in Europe, particularly to Italy where his family and their name had originated many generations earlier. Barnes nodded in reply as his host pointed to the vintage black Mercedes that would take them on the short drive to the main house. The driver – old but considerably younger than Medina – collected the few bags the visitors needed for their overnight stay and stowed these items in the trunk. Inside the car minutes later, they completed the individual introductions, exchanged banalities about the weather, each others' health and similar topics as Barnes listened carefully and watched his elderly host. There was something about his reserved manner, watchful eyes and the careful way in which he selected words to convey even the most fundamental information that informed the younger man that Medina was at least shrewd and probably very smart. "He knows more than he lets on," Barnes thought with more insight than he realized at the time.

Medina, indeed, knew more about Barnes than he let on. He knew his guest was traveling under an alias and was possibly sought by U.S. authorities for an unspecified but serious offense of some kind. He had gotten the information from a ranking official with the Argentine federal police, a man who had alerted him and other large land owners that a fugitive was in the market for a substantial ranch property somewhere in Latin America. The information was sparse and generalized, but it provided a close description of the so called wanted man that matched Barnes down to his over-sized shoes. It also accurately described his three traveling companions and the kind of aircraft he probably had at his disposal. Medina put two and two together and got the right answer.

But the old man cared little about vague allegations from a distant place, preferring to make his own judgment about Barnes and his capacity to buy and successfully run the great ranch. In fact, he thought a resourceful fugitive -- assuming he hadn't done anything morally reprehensible – might prove better equipped to ensure the survival of his holdings than some pedestrian rancher or businessman with more money than imagination. From the first moments of their meeting, consequently, Medina took the measure of Barnes just as Barnes did the same with him.

The meal that evening inevitably centered on Argentine beef, skillfully prepared by Medina's cook and preceded and accompanied by wines from an excellent cellar. Over dinner, the conversation once again was superficial, which allowed Isabella, Diego and Maria to make generalized lies about their individual histories while Medina -- with greater truth and quiet but evident pride – talked about the ranch and his departed family. His wife, they learned, had died years earlier of cancer, and one of his two sons, a naval officer, had been killed in the Falklands war, which Argentina lost to Britain in 1982. The other had died in an automobile accident. A series of other calamities had decimated the Medina family, almost as though some cosmic force had willed its destruction.

Medina was not a man to randomly disclose deeply personal information, but he thought it important that Barnes understood his purpose went beyond the simple sale of property. He wanted him to understand his deep attachment to the land, his desire to preserve the ranch, and to find out if those sentiments meant anything at all to this alien stranger.

"Mr. Cherbic," he said following dinner, knowing the name was an alias, "why don't we have cognac and cigars here, assuming you smoke, while the others have something on the terrace." The implication it was time to discuss business was clear, and Isabella, Diego and Maria excused themselves and were led by a silent young servant, little more than a girl, out French doors into a balmy night.

Medina – who had done military service in his youth – suspected early on that Barnes had been a soldier. His military carriage and other visible aspects of his person had given that background away to less observant people than this cagey old man. Beyond that observation, Medina recognized someone he deemed thoughtful and prudent yet decisive, all qualities he respected. Given these early impressions on his part and something quite reciprocal from Barnes, the two men made immediate progress in their discussion. They talked well into the night, long after Isabella, Diego and Maria had gone to bed and as smoke from their Cuban cigars gradually diffused the flickering candlelight.

Their conversation had been relatively candid, mainly because they skirted certain subjects both men, but particularly Barnes, considered private matters that had nothing to do with the business at hand. Medina wanted to know what Barnes proposed to do with the ranch and if he had the resources and ability to acquire and successfully run it. For his part, Barnes sought information on everything from the asking price for the property to evaluations of the work force. He wanted to know about the short and long term prospects for the business and about the local and national political environment. He asked major questions about the ranch's profitability and operating costs as well as minor ones that revealed he had done a good deal of homework ahead of the meeting. He had even flown an aerial reconnaissance of the entire spread prior to landing earlier that day, and planned to inspect on horseback specific areas of the property before he left the next afternoon. But he revealed nothing of his personal background.

Medina was able to determine from the general tenor of their discussion that Barnes sought a home and not just an investment, although he extracted that impression more from intuition than from anything the younger man said. He put a great deal of stock in intuition because it had served him well over the years, mostly because it was backed with careful observation, prudence and a reasonable understanding of human nature.

"It's late," he finally said to Barnes, "and I'm an old man, which means I don't have the luxury of time I once had." He thought for a moment and continued. "I'm going to be frank with you because I want to pass this ranch on to someone who respects this land and the traditions that go with it." The implication that Barnes could be trusted with that responsibility seemed incredible to him, coming as it did so soon after their first meeting. He was even more surprised when Medina told him about the alert he had received from the federal police. "I know you may be a fugitive from foreign justice," he said, "but my instincts tell me you're an honorable man. I don't even know your real name, but I know more about you than you might imagine."

"I'm not quite a fugitive because there are no actual charges against me," the younger man revealed, "but whatever my status, it has little to do with real justice." Barnes continued to believe he had shot to death two men who had murdered his father, although they were innocent of that particular crime but guilty of others. Had he been privy to all the facts in the case – particularly the venal records of the two dead men – he probably would have chalked it up to justifiable homicide. And the further probability was that Medina would have done the same thing. These two men – very different in appearance and cultural extraction – were quite similar in many other respects. They both cleaved to a simple sense of what they considered honor, and both were independent and resourceful to the point of arrogance. Barnes, it seemed, had discovered an older version of Diego Martinez.

"Given my reported record," he asked the old man as they left the dining table where they had talked the evening away, "weren't you concerned for your safety? For all you know, I could be a serial killer."

The old man smiled and with both hands gently exposed two pistol grips on both sides of the belt he wore under a light linen jacket. "I trust you with my property, but not my life," he said, not entirely in jest. "If I retain my life, I can always reclaim my property." Barnes realized they were even more alike than he was beginning to suspect.

*

Chapter Five

Sonny Spivak was an attorney who made corrupt lawyers look good by comparison. Although his wasn't an acute legal mind, he was reasonably competent in a professional sense. He had sufficient intelligence and more than his share of shrewdness for the conduct of a decent legal practice. But his ethical standards had over the years been so appalling that members of the local bar association considered him something between a scoundrel and an outright crook.

Spivak had built a thriving law practice defending many of the community's most notorious criminals and was generally considered a mob lawyer, although he was perfectly willing to represent slumlords, embezzlers, pimps and a variety of hustlers and other social outcasts so long as they could pay his fees in one form or another. He drove a Rolls-Royce Phantom that had once belonged to one of his clients and seemed unaware that the car was entirely disproportionate to his otherwise rather modest lifestyle. He lived in a two-bedroom, downtown apartment only blocks from his office but a distance he drove because he liked to display his expensive automobile and because he hated exercise in any form. That inclination was apparent in the softness of his round face and a waistline that was gradually expanding as he approached his fifties. Other than the Rolls and a 40-foot yacht, also acquired from a financially distressed client and moored at a marina for power boats on Lake Millstone, his only indulgences were the expensively tailored suits and shirts he wore to no good effect. Despite the cost, his clothes were usually rumpled and often bore evidence of a recent meal.

Spivak's long-suffering wife had divorced him several years earlier, fed up with his incessant infidelities with prostitutes and morally pliable secretaries. She had found him in his office one afternoon, naked with only a young blonde woman, equally bare, between him and his soft leather couch. "I'll be with you in a minute," he said to his wife only moments before she slammed the door and went down the hall to see another attorney about a divorce.

Spivak had no illusions about his physical qualities but had learned early in adult life there were women – some of them quite attractive – perfectly willing to provide all the sex he wanted for money. Since he had only confused sex with love once in his life, the arrangement struck him as almost ideal. There was no need to waste time with everything from courtship to domestic chores, only the obligatory payment after climax and nothing more. Given this knowledge and a sufficient supply of cash, Spivak was able to indulge his rapacious appetite for sex, often on the office couch where clients had been seated somewhat earlier and others would sit not long afterward. Had any of them bothered to notice, the subtle wear pattern on the Italian leather seats suggested the furniture had been employed more as a bed than anything else. The horny lawyer also used it for his regular afternoon naps.

Despite his Rolls-Royce and the yacht – which he had learned to pilot but rarely used – Spivak was an exceptionally frugal man. "Cheap," in fact, was the word often employed by those who knew him, particularly the servers in the restaurants where he ate with regularity or the dozens of others who did small business with him on a regular basis. He even had a reputation for cheapness among his criminal clients, who tolerated his behavior because he was an effective attorney and also because it amused many of them. Most had learned that Spivak's frugality even extended to the small bar he maintained in his office, where incredibly cheap whiskies and other beverages had been put into bottles that once contained only the most expensive brands. He had not even bothered to buy the original bottles, acquiring empties where he could and personally refilling the containers with a small glass funnel he kept for the purpose.

There was the general assumption among those who knew Spivak in a casual way that his lack of polish and cheapness derived from a poor childhood, one that accounted for his absence of style and near miserly behavior. But the few who knew him well understood that was not the case. His father had been a successful merchant and the son had grown up in an affluent suburban environment. Although his academic record had only been good enough to get him into law school, Spivak had graduated a well-regarded state university and his father had financed his entire education. The long-dead father, in fact, had been rather generous, not only to his small family but to friends, various needy individuals and a number of local charities. In other words, the lawyer's profound deficiencies were neither the product of immediate heredity nor environment, which suggests that human nature is quite mysterious and that its sources are not always apparent.

"Christ on a bloody crutch," Spivak said, pulling on his pants as Price entered the office. And as he zipped the fly and buckled his belt, he beckoned the detective to have the seat that only moments before had served as a drying rack for his water-soaked trousers. He had been working at his desk in his underwear, but saw no reason to explain that circumstance to Price, who assumed correctly that the situation was somehow related to the day-long, steady rain that pounded against the office windows.

"What now?" Spivak inquired, referring to earlier interrogations Price had conducted with him in connection with the murder of Albert Moretti, a former law client and one of the men Toby Barnes had shot to avenge his father. He noticed that Price had not taken a seat and that his expression was less than friendly.

"Now," Price said at last, "I want some real information or we're going to have a real problem." Spivak had dealt with tough men and difficult situations over his entire career and was not entirely intimidated by this burly intruder, but he also knew Price's reputation for directness, physical and otherwise, and was cautious enough not to aggravate him beyond his present annoyance.

"If you're talking about Moretti," the lawyer replied, "I've told you everything I know." Actually, he had told Price more than he knew. He had inadvertently related both murder victims to the same home town when he casually mentioned that Moretti had originally come from Clarendon. That isolated bit of information had set Price and McCurdy on a trail that had greatly illuminated the case.

Price planted both of his big fists menacingly on Spivak's desk and came to the point. "Moretti is history," he said. "I know you alerted Barnes to my arrival in the Virgin Islands, and I know you've had some half-assed private investigator on my case. I want to know where Barnes is, and I want you to call off your hound."

Spivak, who chose his words carefully, pointed out that Barnes was his client and to his knowledge no criminal charges had been brought against him. And as far as the investigator was concerned, he added, there was nothing illegal or unethical about the work he had done.

"You're not listening," Price said with a distinct edge to his voice that conveyed a message beyond those implied by the words. "I'm not here for a god-damn debate. I want to know where to find Toby Barnes and I want you to fire that snoop."

Vaguely aware his pants were still damp, Spivak gave Price's demand momentary thought and came up with one of his characteristic evasions. "I don't know where Barnes is now and couldn't find him if my life depended on it," he lied with a perfectly straight face, "but I'll call off the investigator, not because I fear anything from you but because he's already served his purpose." The part about not fearing Price wasn't entirely true.

Price had not expected to learn anything from Spivak, but wanted him to know his intrusion into the case had not gone unnoticed and would probably attract some kind of retribution if he continued the offense. He had also been annoyed by the surveillance placed on him by the lawyer, considering it a violation of both his professional and personal privacy and only marginally aware he had done exactly the same thing to hundreds of others over his long career.

"Don't make me come back," Price advised as he turned and went to the door.

“Is that a threat?” Spivak asked, implying there might be some legal remedy if that was the case.

“Consider it a friendly suggestion,” Price replied and left, not closing the heavy door behind him. Spivak, relieved to see him go and uncomfortable in his damp pants, watched the detective depart through the outer office and another door as he pondered the meeting and its likely effect, if any, on his affairs. Not much, he concluded before he removed his trousers again, draped the garment on the same chair and returned in his underwear, red boxer shorts, to desk work he had begun before Price’s arrival. But there was a lingering question that puzzled him. The detective had no raincoat or umbrella, yet was perfectly dry, a circumstance that would have been almost impossible in the driving rain even if someone had delivered him by car to the curb outside the building entrance. It was just another one of those imponderables, he finally decided, and went on with his work.

Price had not expected to extract anything in the way of specific information from Spivak, but their brief meeting convinced him the lawyer had some mechanism for contacting Barnes on matters of importance. He thought it unlikely the cagey Barnes would reveal much in the way of personal information, particularly his location, to someone as disreputable as Spivak, which suggested there was probably an intermediate contact. That contact, Price speculated, would likely be someone Barnes would trust; someone, perhaps, in his own family.

Barnes had only one surviving relative, his mother’s sister, a fact Price knew from early on in the investigation. Her name was Sally Crapper, a respected school teacher in Clarendon, the small town where Barnes had lived with his parents for the first five years of his life and where his father, also a teacher, had been shot to death. Price knew, too, that Barnes had made financial provisions for his aunt, and that she had been in recent contact with him. Some of the information he had assembled on Sally Crapper came from Jack McCurdy, who had stumbled into an intimate relationship with the woman in the course of conducting an interview with her some months earlier.

McCurdy had gone to Clarendon when he and Price learned the two murder victims, Albert Moretti and Fred Quinn, were from the same town, a circumstance that could have been coincidence but one, they thought, that needed further scrutiny. In the course of the investigation, McCurdy had managed to not only get involved with Sally Crapper but with another woman, Clarette Barlow, as well. His steamy collisions with these two principals in the case – carried out mostly in the course of a single day – alerted him to energies he didn't know he had, but also signaled his wife, who found lipstick smudges on one of his shirts, to a situation she found intolerable. She tossed him out of the household and later allowed him to return, humbled, on terms that precluded any further trips to Clarendon.

Later, Price learned that Clarette Barlow, who had known both murder victims in high school, had probably been raped as a teenager by Chester Barnes, her teacher and Toby's father, and had more than likely shot her molester to death in an act of revenge. Albert Moretti, who for reasons only he knew had changed his name from Simmons, gave her the gun but was innocent of the actual crime. The sheriff who investigated the case 20 years earlier had at least an inkling of what had happened, but assumed Chester Barnes got what he deserved and there was not sufficient evidence to prosecute the young woman. She, meanwhile, went on to become head of the surgical nursing program at the local hospital as well as a formidable, although temporary, sex partner for Jack McCurdy.

Essentially a straight forward person, McCurdy wasn't schooled enough in deception to keep these affairs from either his wife, Missy, or from Price, who read his friend like a best-selling novel. Detective that he was, he deduced that McCurdy had been multiply laid and later learned from McCurdy himself that his wife had not only discovered his infidelities and thrown him out, but taken him back on condition there were no more improprieties. Price was close to the McCurdys and had no desire to further jeopardize their marriage, but he also realized Jack was in a unique position to secure information from Sally Crapper about her nephew, Toby Barnes. The trick, he figured, was to convince McCurdy to see the woman, talk to her and let it go at that. It was a little like walking a tightrope across a windy canyon, but it was worth a try.

McCurdy, on the other hand, thought it was a bad idea when Price proposed it at lunch following his testy confrontation with Sonny Spivak. Their meeting at The Bristol Bar and Grill had not been arranged for any particular purpose, but Price made the suggestion as soon as they had seated themselves in a back booth.

"Jesus," McCurdy said, "are you trying to wreck what's left of my marriage?"

"I know it's a lot to ask, but there's no reason Missy has to know you've seen this woman," Price replied. "Your only challenge would be to keep your fly zipped and get out of there after the meeting." He knew a trip to Clarendon was out of the question for McCurdy, but thought he might invite Sally Crapper to the city on some flimsy pretext. He understood that this woman – unlike Clarette Barlow who had expected more of their relationship – bore McCurdy no ill will and might conceivably welcome the invitation. If nothing else, Price reasoned, it would give her an excuse to get out of Clarendon for a few hours. City born and bred, the detective assumed most small town residents needed an occasional change of scene. He was a man who had never seen wheat in a field.

McCurdy genuinely loved his wife and had meant his recent promise of future fidelity, but there was a lingering attraction to Sally Crapper that lurked somewhere beyond his conscious recognition. He had enjoyed the unions with both women in Clarendon and had thought of them in those dark moments at night before sleep, but Sally had been the predominant image, perhaps because her nature was softer and more forgiving than was the case with the vituperative nurse, Clarette Barlow. He could more easily reconstruct the memory of their time together because there had been no bitter words to interfere with the recollection.

Price knew nothing of his friend's inner thoughts, of course, but he intuitively sensed that McCurdy was still attracted to Sally Crapper and he was not above using that attraction to gain what he considered a justifiable end. He saw no abrogation of their friendship in his willingness to risk McCurdy's marriage to further an investigation, which only proved he was about as sensitive as an old wrestler's sock.

As The Bristol began to fill with its mainly regular group of lunch customers – most of them soaked from the continuing rain – the two men continued an off-and-on discussion of what Price began to call "The Sally Finale." He told McCurdy that something as simple as an intimate discussion with the woman might disclose information that was probably not available from any other source. Price not only wanted to know where Barnes was but where he planned to go, and needed something that would tie the man conclusively to the two murders. Sally Crapper, he told McCurdy again and again, although in different ways, was the most direct link to their principal suspect.

"I assume you're going to pay for lunch because I don't have any money," McCurdy said at last, "but that doesn't give you the right to ruin my digestion." He thought for a moment and added: "Or my marriage." But there was something in his tone that told Price his cause was not lost. McCurdy, he realized, was considering the proposal.

"Why don't you think it over," Price suggested as they finished their food, "but not too long." McCurdy made no commitment, either to thought or action, but it was apparent to his friend that he had taken the matter under advisement. That meant, Price knew, he would do nothing at all unless there was relentless pursuit of the proposal. McCurdy, he also knew, was a decisive police officer, but the world's worst malingerer when it came to dicey personal decisions. He simply put those issues out of his mind unless someone harassed him to action. In this case, Price was that someone.

"I'll give it some thought," McCurdy agreed as they parted and went separate ways for the afternoon. The logic of Price's argument as it related to the Barnes case had very little bearing on that thought. McCurdy began to recall in precise detail the contours of Sally Crapper's maturing but shapely form. He remembered her passionate little gasps at what he considered appropriate moments, and her apparent satisfaction at the end result. These thoughts eventually overwhelmed his earlier resolve to marital fidelity and he began to wonder if he could recover something of his relationship with Sally and maintain his marriage at the same time. Was it possible, he wondered, to have his cake and eat it, too?

Spivak knew Price's reputation for bending both the rules and the laws when it suited his purpose. He knew the detective was unpredictable and dangerous from his point of view, but he had dealt with cold-blooded killers, various kinds of thugs and a host of other disreputable types in the course of a long and mainly successful law practice, and decided he was not going to be intimidated by some cop whose basic instincts resembled those of his clients. "Screw that bastard," he thought, but only after the alleged bastard had left his presence and presented no immediate threat.

Spivak said he would call off the private detective hired to monitor Price's activities and had actually tinkered with the idea of keeping that promise. Instead, he decided to use another agency and to make certain they operated with more discretion than the one whose surveillance had been so easily detected and had led to confrontation with the cantankerous Price. He understood there was an element of risk in continuing the surveillance, but Barnes had paid him generously for the tip that enabled him to escape the Virgin Islands and there was the real possibility of additional revenues from that same source for information on Price's activities. Given that prospect, Spivak negotiated an arrangement with the best private investigator in town, Frank Tingle.

Tingle was a man of considerable substance, both in his physical and professional presence. He weighed more than 320 pounds and was easily the smartest person in a local field not known for its intellectual giants. His abundant size would have been enough to attract attention, but he also cultivated a bushy red mustache and dressed in a style that would have been described as "natty" in an earlier time. Given his size, it took a competent tailor and quality materials to achieve that effect.

Tingle's robust dimensions disguised for those who didn't know him a natural athleticism that had once made him an All-American lineman at the state university and a skilled ballroom dancer. The big man loved to dance and his considerable ability in that regard and a certain innate charm enabled him to achieve more success with women than one might expect from someone of his great size.

Frank Tingle & Associates was a firm composed of Frank Tingle and his secretary, office manager and general confidant, Lily Smith, who had worked for him the 15 years since his firing from the police force for reasons never disclosed to the public or, for that matter, his fellow officers. Most of them assumed his transgression had something to do with dirty money and he had been discharged rather than charged because there had not been sufficient proof to do otherwise. But that was rumor and Tingle was not inclined to comment on those circumstances, either then or later.

An exceptionally good police officer in the professional if not the ethical sense, Tingle soon built a successful business based on the skills and contacts he had developed on the force. His clients eventually included some of the largest corporations in the city as well as women, usually wealthy, who sought to gain sufficient evidence against philandering husbands to achieve substantial divorce settlements. He invariably delivered the goods his clients sought, and Sonny Spivak was well aware of Tingle's solid reputation. But there was something Spivak didn't know, and it would soon cause him a good deal of trouble.

Although they did not see much of one another, Frank Tingle and Bill Price were old friends. They had been rookies together on the police force, and Tingle remembered that Price had stood by him during the difficult period of his dismissal, a time when other friends and associates had avoided him like a bum with body odor. Price had also directed some small business his way when he first set up shop, and Tingle now returned the favor by accepting Spivak as a client with the intention of revealing all he could learn to Price. There was a huge ethical flaw in his behavior, Tingle fully realized, but his obligation to Price was a matter of honor.

*

Chapter Six

The evidence against Toby Barnes in the murder of Albert Moretti, born Albert Simmons, was entirely circumstantial until the father of a 14-year-old witness, many months after the event, dramatically altered the case. His son and a teenage friend didn't see the actual shooting, but they saw the killer escape the building and, more importantly, dispose of a bag that held a disassembled .50 caliber rifle, tripod and several other incriminating items. The boys had been in the alley, clandestinely smoking some forbidden substance, when the killer made his exit and stuffed the bag into a rusting old dumpster not far from the deserted building. The shot that ended Moretti's criminal career had been made from the roof of that structure.

The testimony of both boys not only enabled the police to recover the weapon and other evidence, but gave them eye-witness descriptions of either Toby Barnes or an identical twin. They had seen him from not more than a dozen feet away and both had made separate identifications from photographs supplied by the authorities. Barnes had not seen them, crouched as they were in a nearby doorway that had been unused for many years.

The boys learned of the shooting that same day and realized they had seen the killer make his escape. But they were reluctant to disclose this information to either the police or their parents. They had been engaged in their own illegal activity and the man they saw leave that building had a substantial presence that lingered in their minds. He was not only big and powerful looking, but the expression on his face, although fleetingly witnessed, appeared fearsome to the two young witnesses.

They decided to keep the matter a secret between them, a vow that lasted for some months until one of them was caught smoking that same prohibited substance by his father and inadvertently told the parent what he had seen in an effort to evade his more current dilemma. A good citizen, the father alerted the police who, in turn, recovered the evidence that soon made Toby Barnes a real fugitive from justice rather than merely a person of interest in the case.

"We've finally nailed that elusive son-of-a-bitch," Price told Diana as they sat at the bar in The Bristol. It was early on a weekday evening and they had met for what had become a customary pre-dinner drink.

"I wouldn't say you've exactly nailed him," Diana replied. "There isn't anyone in plain sight who knows where he is, and they probably wouldn't be able to catch him if they did." She poked delicately with her stirrer at the lemon twist in her drink. It was vodka on the rocks.

"Maybe so, but now he's part of my official workload and not just a hobby," he said. The case had been reactivated based on the new evidence and the sure knowledge a warrant for the arrest of Toby Barnes was inevitable.

Price led the investigation instigated by discovery of the young witnesses and realized immediately the case had taken a turn that provided him with new options in what had previously seemed a futile search effort. He had operated before without official sanction and with limited resources in an effort to find a clever killer with almost unlimited resources and extensive international experience and contacts. Now, he had not only gained the open support of his own police department and similar organizations around the nation and globe, but other means as well to find Toby Barnes.

As they sat at the bar, he revealed to Diana that his old friend, Frank Tingle, now retained as a private investigator by Sonny Spivak, would serve as a conduit for information sent to Barnes. "I can control that information and, perhaps, get him to do something foolish," Price explained. "I may even be able to find him if that creep, Sonny Spivak, is a little careless when he contacts his client." He was reasonably confident those contacts were routed through Sally Crapper, which explained his effort to get Jack McCurdy to revisit the woman. There was little chance, he knew, that a local judge would approve a wiretap on Spivak's phones since there was no evidence he had done anything illegal. And even if they were able to secure a wiretap, the veteran mob attorney was unlikely to divulge anything on an open line. The probable option, Price thought, was that the two, Spivak and Crapper, met on those rare occasions when the attorney had important information for Barnes. Or, perhaps, Spivak used some third party for the meetings with his client's aunt. Was there a chance the attorney might employ his new private investigator for that purpose, he wondered? The possibilities in the investigation were beginning to expand.

"Are you interested in pictures of the fugitive?" Price asked Diana, who had been reading a dinner menu as he speculated to himself on the case. His reference was to a series of newspaper photographs taken of Barnes in the Ozarks and sent to him by the local sheriff, Jesse Jones. The pictures had been made by the owner, editor and sole staff member of the local newspaper and were occasioned by the big man's participation in a number of civic and charitable activities when he lived in the area.

"You bet," she said, putting the menu aside as he anticipated her response and retrieved a small stack of black and white prints from a business case he had put on the floor at the base of his stool. She took the photographs and placed them before her on the bar, careful to avoid the damp spot created by her drink.

"We showed these pictures to the boys who saw Barnes near the murder scene," he said, pointing out that the photographer had caught the man in a wide variety of poses, some close up and others from near distance. Diana slowly examined the material, noting in particular a man shown next to Barnes in several of the shots. "Who's this?" she asked.

"That's his trusted sidekick, Diego Martinez," Price replied. "A man of considerable mystery and apparently quite indispensable to his boss. As far as his background is concerned, we, meaning the authorities, don't have a clue."

As she examined and reexamined the photographs, some element of recognition registered in her mind but she couldn't come immediately to a conclusion. She had not known Diego's name at the time of their entanglement in the Central American jungle and he was only a late teenager at the time. She had known a good-looking but bedraggled rebel and the pictures that confronted her in the Stockton newspaper showed a mature, well-groomed man with a persistent expression of restrained confidence. "Who in hell is this guy?" she thought, rummaging silently through her recollections for an answer.

That answer came to her later that same night when she awoke from a deep sleep with the instant realization – derived from some mysterious and unexplainable source – that her jungle lover and the man in the newspaper photographs were one and the same person. "Jesus God," she exclaimed, and shook Price, slumbering next to her, awake to disclose the revelation. She modified that disclosure, however, to exclude her sexual romp with the young rebel, revealing only that he had been one of the group, although a kind one, that had kidnapped her in Central America many years earlier. She felt no shame about her relationship with Diego, only the notion it was a private matter that had nothing to do with Price or anyone else.

"Are you sure?" Price asked, once he had shaken off the disorientation of his abrupt awakening and understood what she had told him. The information, he soon realized, might serve to fill in some of the many blanks in the Barnes file. His connection with Martinez more than likely originated in Central America, the detective reasoned once Diana had described for him the hard life the rebels had endured. It was unlikely a poor man in his circumstances would have found his way to the Ozarks on his own, which suggested that Barnes had somehow met him in his native land. It was conjecture of the broadest kind, but it was another lead and Price began to sense that he was making real progress in the case. Earlier, the lack of progress would have discouraged others, but not him. He had an internal mechanism -- probably developed over time – that discounted obstacles and kept him going until it was absolutely clear there was no place to go.

Diana's realization that her first lover was not only alive, but mature and associated somehow with the notorious Toby Barnes seemed to her a coincidence that would have been entirely unacceptable in a work of fiction. Her initial reaction was one of ambivalence, but she soon decided there were interesting implications in the situation. She was curious about Diego, and wanted to know more about the circumstances that had delivered him, little more than a boy, from that dangerous jungle to his present circumstances. She had no amorous inclinations toward the man, but there were residual feelings of fondness for the brief but intense moments they had shared so long ago.

Price, on the other hand, wanted to know about the history and locale of the insurrection as well as anything Diana remembered about the rebels, particularly the one she had identified. He understood she was only a girl at the time and probably knew little about the political or her geographical situation, but she did provide snippets of recollection he eventually translated into useful information. He wanted to know what Barnes was doing in Central America when he met Diego Martinez, assuming that was the case. The answer to that question, he correctly surmised, could well shed light on important events in the story he was systematically piecing together.

Although not that day or the next, Diana's identification of Diego Martinez and his geographic origins would eventually inform Price on the source of the great wealth Toby Barnes had assembled, not seemingly but actually, overnight. The detective made a number of assumptions based mainly on simple common sense that supplied the probable explanation, although absolute proof was another matter. Still, his conclusions brought the mysterious fugitive into closer focus and supplied more insight into his complicated personality.

Price had isolated the time frame in which Barnes left the army and reappeared some time later a wealthy man. He assumed the former sergeant had somehow used his military experience to profitable effect, and it seemed likely there had been action of some sort in the general region where Diego Martinez had fought his own little war. That action, Price figured, was probably unique in the sense it had nothing to do with the local political differences. There was little money to be made from such a small scale enterprise, either from the government or the rebels.

The most likely explanation came weeks after Diana identified Diego, and when Price, rummaging through news and other accounts of Central American military and similar activities in a particular time period, came across several articles on the rumored destruction of a large drug cartel. The material was generalized and inconclusive, based on information from indigenous and other unofficial sources, but all accounts attributed the assault not to a rival gang but to some unknown but powerful military force. The drug lord and his organization had disappeared overnight along with their presumptive wealth.

"I think these rumors are largely true," Price said to Diana on still another night at The Bristol where he had disclosed his new theory to her as they sat, chatting amicably, at the bar. "There aren't many other ways he could have amassed the kind of money he has with his background. Barnes is neither an investment banker nor one of the world's great entrepreneurs, but he is a trained killer and a good one." The rumors, Price told her, suggested the drug people had been dispatched with deadly precision, a form of primitive justice that reminded him of the Moretti and Quinn killings. "I think our man Barnes is a hard case," he continued. "He killed the men he thought killed his father, and he killed those two murdering bastards in the Ozarks. And he more than likely killed that mysterious drug kingpin and his men in Central America and no telling how many others in his Special Forces military career. As far as sheer numbers are concerned, he could have depopulated a good sized small town.

"He gets trash off the streets," Diana replied, not entirely in jest.

"There's some truth to that," Price admitted, "but I've lost my sympathy for the man. I think honest retribution is a noble enterprise in moderation, but this guy has gone off the deep end. He's going to do some real damage if he's not careful." Price had changed his mind about Barnes. Originally, he thought the Moretti and Quinn murders had some justification, although that had been an entirely personal notion at odds with his position as a sworn law officer. But he understood that a man like Barnes would seek vengeance for the murder of his father, even though he killed two innocent men in the process. What, Price wondered, would Barnes have done had he known his father was a raper of teenage girls?

Somewhat later, they had eaten dinner at the bar and Price had gone to the men's room, more to wash his hands than anything else. On his return, he found a stranger sitting on his barstool in an apparent attempt to engage Diana in conversation. Her crisp, evasive manner told him immediately the man was neither a friend nor an acquaintance. "No," she told the intruder, "I don't know Nancy Belvedere and I've never been to the South Oaks Hunt Club. Not only that," she added, "I don't want to know Nancy what's-her-name and I'd rather piss up a rope than go to the South Oaks Hunt Club."

Undeterred by the frosty reception, the man was about to take another approach when Price grasp the sleeve of his cashmere jacket, jerked him from the barstool into a standing position, and stepped heavily on the toe of his shoe. "One word from you," he said, as the man simultaneously expressed both surprise and pain, "and I'll deck your scrawny ass." Actually, the man was somewhat larger than Price and his ass was far from scrawny, but he got the message and fled the bar as soon as the pressure was released from his smashed shoe.

"You're kind of cute," Diana observed, as Price regained his stool and ordered another drink from the bartender, who knew his customer well and had been waiting to see what would happen when he returned from the men's room. And what happened was pretty much what he had expected to happen.

Later that night, Diana lay awake after what she and Price had done what she and Diego Martinez had done years before in the Central American jungle. She had no doubt about her attachment to the middle-aged man who slept at her side, but she had an almost maternal concern for the young one, now fully mature, she had barely known. She had thought him long dead and mostly forgotten until she saw the pictures in the Ozark newspaper. Afterward, she felt renewed, somehow, by the knowledge he was not only alive but quite well. She had no desire to confront him, knowing their time together was mainly hormonal and they had nothing else to her knowledge in common.

"What could I say to him?" she thought, as sleep began to descend on her. “Nice screw. Sorry it had to end so soon.” His occupation of her thoughts was understandable, given the recent discovery he still lived, but she now had concerns about his future. She knew Price was more determined than ever to track Barnes down, and she began to fear that his pursuit would one day put him into direct conflict with the fugitive’s right-hand man, her first lover. And while Price was her main concern, she was troubled by that prospect.

*

Chapter Seven

Toby Barnes had been favorably impressed with the Medina ranch and its owner, but simple prudence demanded he also inspect other properties before making a final decision in what would amount to the investment of many millions of dollars. He said as much to Oscar Medina before he and his party – Isabella, Diego and Maria – flew off the long private airstrip on a sunny afternoon, the steady surge of twin turbo-prop engines providing accompaniment to the splendid view of broad grasslands expanding below them as they climbed to cruising altitude. Barnes, alone at the controls, had spent the morning inspecting everything from ranch animals and equipment to the hardy men who worked the spread. The operation was substantial – much larger than the Ozark ranch – and Barnes realized he had a good deal to learn before he made a decision, one way or the other, about the purchase. But he liked what he had seen and was inclined at that time to place it high on his list of prospects. The price, while substantial, was realistic and the only unusual provision was the one that allowed Medina, at 80, to live out his life in a small house he had built for that purpose on the property.

Barnes had wondered if the old man would be content to idle away his declining years or would from long habit meddle in ranch affairs. "I suppose," he joked to himself, "I could shoot the old boy if he caused trouble, unless, of course, he shot me first." He recalled the pistols Medina carried at dinner the previous evening and had a further thought made possible by his ability to appreciate irony. He had evaded death scores of times in as many places at the hands of strong, determined adversaries. "I wouldn't be surprised if some frail, old man finally got the job done," Barnes thought, knowing from first hand observation that death often came as a surprise to the recipient. He had not only seen that surprised look, but had been its cause on a number of occasions.

But his attention was focused on the plane as he took a compass heading north, piloting the aircraft as his passengers relaxed with their individual thoughts in the cabin behind him. Isabella had persuaded Barnes to give them a short holiday in Rio de Janeiro, a break she welcomed from the long flights to remote places. She was a person with strong work habits and this extended period of inactivity had begun to bore her. The holiday would be no substitute for real work, but it would at least provide an urban setting for new activities.

Maria, too, anticipated the trip to Rio, although she was far from bored by the incessant travel. She found it interesting and a splendid departure from the narrow life she had led as a girl and a welcome addition to the improvements she had experienced with Diego. He, however, was neither bored nor excited by their extended travel, accepting it as part of the life he had been fortunate enough to gain despite early prospects that were grim to lethal. Although he had an intense romantic attachment to Maria, Diego's fortunes and allegiance were strongly tied to Barnes. The two men in a relatively short period of time had been through more turmoil together than most others, excluding military combat veterans, were likely to experience in their entire lives.

Diego had participated in the assault on the drug lord's fortified mountain and, earlier, had with his rebel band extricated Barnes and his men from the jungle ambush. And he had been with the former Special Forces sergeant when he exacted revenge on the corrupt police official who had leaked information that made the ambush possible.

The police official had feigned cooperation with the military planners who had dispatched Barnes and his Special Forces team to intercept an enormous drug shipment bound for the United States. But that official had long been in the pay of the dominant drug lord, Zee, a fact that became obvious to Barnes once he had survived the ambush. There was little he could do about it at the time, given his Army status, but he was not one to forgive that kind of treachery and he took his revenge after he left service and had accomplished the destruction of Zee and his fortress.

He returned with Diego, who was familiar with the small Central American town where the police official commanded a provincial detachment, and confronted the man who had almost sponsored his death. "Do you know who I am?" he inquired in Spanish of the colonel, who was uncharacteristically alone in his office on an evening his men had been relieved to attend a locally important fiesta in the town square. "No," the man replied, aware the gun pointed in his direction was, in any event, bad news. Barnes patiently identified himself, told the officer his intention, and then put a bullet hole in the center of the man's forehead from short range. He had made certain his betrayer understood the circumstances, and then left his police superiors to puzzle over motive for the execution. Given the man's long and devious career, there were too many possibilities and the authorities eventually relegated the matter to a soon forgotten file. Barnes, too, soon forgot the incident as he accumulated other homicides and commenced work on his Ozark ranch.

Diego, who for years had fought both military and police in his homeland, saw only justice in the cool assassination, and assumed then and later that Barnes was an honorable man who only killed when it was mandated by honor or necessity. He backed without question the man who had delivered him from an interminable, dirty little war that would surely have killed him sooner of later. The women, Isabella and Maria, knew little about the killings, although they, of course, realized there were reasons for their incessant and clandestine travel. Barnes never lied to them about the general situation, but he also never bothered to explain the difficulties that were beginning to accumulate around him. "Time to go" or "The climate is heating up" were often the only indications he gave that it was time to leave wherever they were at the time.

In the beginning, Isabella was intrigued by her large, mysterious and extraordinarily wealthy lover and willingly left her successful business career and previous life behind to live on his Ozark ranch and, later, flee from one mainly luxurious destination to another. The combination of romance and rapidly changing scenery had great initial appeal for her, but the novelty eventually wore away and she began to miss the career she had made in commercial real estate and related enterprises. She had been instrumental in putting together the large land parcels that eventually comprised the Ozark ranch, but had relatively little work to occupy her bright mind and energetic habits since completion of that project. Barnes intended to use her considerable experience and abilities in the acquisition of a new property, but his status first as an elusive suspect and then as a fugitive made it increasingly more difficult to find a suitable place.

Barnes and his party were in Rio when he learned from one of his many sources an arrest warrant had been issued for him in connection with the murder of Albert Moretti, nee Simmons. He kept the information to himself, mostly to allow Isabella an opportunity to enjoy the brief holiday before they began what he knew would be an even more determined effort to disappear than the one that had led to her current disenchantment. She had not voiced her dissatisfaction, but Barnes was no fool, even where women were concerned, and he sensed from her increasingly distant behavior that their relationship was in some stage of dissolution. This knowledge was mildly painful to him, but he was not one to crumble under the weight of a failed romance or anything else. And the arrest warrant had given him a more immediate problem with implications, he felt, that were far more serious than a break-up with Isabella.

Rio de Janeiro, with its splendid harbor surrounded by low mountain ranges, is, like so many great metropolitan centers around the world, a study in contrasts. The opulence and comforts afforded by great wealth were present not far from the many favellas or slums where the desperately poor and crime afflicted lived in squalor. Barnes was aware of this anomaly – not just in Rio but in many other cities – and it was one reason he sought the insulation of open space, the kind afforded by great ranches and vast stretches of his own land. As Isabella, Diego and Maria enjoyed the amenities of a first class hotel and other cosmopolitan pleasures, Barnes pondered his next move. He had not yet discounted acquisition of the Medina ranch, although he suspected his presence in that region would soon be detected and would close out that possibility. "Where to, now?" he thought as the outline of a plan slowly emerged from somewhere in his sub-conscious mind.

At about the same time, Isabella had similar thoughts, but ones that were completely divergent from those of her companion. She had not only decided to leave Barnes, but knew she would return to Chicago to resume the former life and career she now missed with something a little short of desperation. The only problem was revealing that intention to Barnes, a man she still regarded with great affection, if not the amorous intensity that had originally dominated their relationship.

"I know," Barnes told her as they sat comfortably on the balcony of their hotel suite and gazed at the darkening waters of the distant bay. She had managed to disclose her plan and was surprised to learn he was not surprised.

"I would like to remain more than your friend," she said with sincerity but aware her words had the ring of a break-up platitude.

"If you mean it," he replied, "I can get to Chicago as easily as anywhere else. But I think there's something you need to know before you extend me an open invitation." He told her about the arrest warrant and the muddling effect it would surely have on his future affairs, and suggested she might want to reconsider her offer to continue the relationship, although on a somewhat altered basis. He was a fugitive and would likely remain one for a long time, he warned.

"That doesn't bother me," Isabella said. "We've been fugitives together these past months." She sipped her wine as a soft breeze ruffled tropical plants in terra cotta pots near them. "It's been wonderful in many ways, but I can't live on romance. I have to work and use romance as a diversion . . . or the romance doesn't work."

"I understand that, too," Barnes replied, realizing they had reached a divide in their relationship, but pleased it had been amicable and would probably continue in a diminished form. He suggested and she agreed that they finish the week in Rio while he arranged private jet transportation for her to Chicago. As it turned out, the plan was a good one for reasons beyond their changing personal circumstances.

Barnes correctly assumed the authorities had issued bulletins that fully described him, his traveling companions and their plane. He rendered those descriptions useless before their departure from Rio by disposal of the aircraft, dispersal of their group and a personal disguise that changed everything about him except one permanent feature, his great height. "I suppose I could have myself surgically shortened," he told Isabella before she boarded her plane to the United States, "but I've come to enjoy the view from up here." The view was the same but his appearance was quite different. He had dyed his sand-colored hair black and his beard, only two days old at the time, soon grew longer and received a neat trim. He wore round, wire-rimmed spectacles with plain glass and modified his ramrod posture somewhat in an effort to minimize his size and to deconstruct the military bearing that had often telegraphed to careful observers his former occupation. It wasn't perfect, he knew, but there was only so much that could be done with someone of his proportions.

At the end of the week in Rio, Diego and Maria returned to Costa Rica where they had acquired a home in a geographical setting that reminded them of their native country. They made the trip in the first class section of a commercial flight with meticulously crafted false passports and other documentation Barnes had earlier assembled for them as a precaution that eventually turned into a real need. Diego understood he would join his friend again in some enterprise once things had settled, and he was given the means to circuitously contact Barnes, but only in a true emergency.

In the Argentine, meanwhile, Oscar Medina received word from Barnes that he was not in a position to purchase the ranch, either then or, in all probability, later. Barnes told him the essential truth without a great deal of detail, and thanked the old man for his hospitality. For his part, Medina genuinely regretted the news. He had sought not only a buyer for the property, but something of a surrogate heir in the absence of his own family. "You are always welcome here," he told Barnes, a man he had only known for a day but one he had, never-the-less, come to like and respect. And for his part, Barnes, although suspicious by nature and experience, sensed he had a real friend in Oscar Medina and that the invitation was genuine.

Barnes remained in Rio for a couple of weeks longer to complete financial and other arrangements that gave him a variety of travel options. The additional time also produced a fuller beard - part of his new identity - and still another name, Juan Caldera. The new pose cast the former sergeant as an American of Latin descent, which he thought necessary to explain his imperfect Spanish and his accent in that language. He also used the time to tweak his new disguise, testing it in restaurants and other public places before putting it to the ultimate test on national frontiers as he traveled through various countries. And he sold the plane through a shady broker for much less than its actual value, although at a price substantial enough to turn what could have been a total loss into, considering the circumstances, a reasonable recovery.

The tall, phony Latino then boarded a commercial flight with a single carry-on bag and kept to himself as much as possible, sleeping or feigning sleep in an uncomfortable coach seat as the plane flew north into gathering darkness. Through strategic bribes, he had dispatched another bag, stowed in the same aircraft, that contained funds in several currencies as well as important papers and his .45 caliber Glock auto pistol. His immediate destination was New York, where he intended to rent a car and drive to Chicago for a brief reunion with Isabella. They had planned the meeting for both personal and business reasons and also because Barnes assumed the last place authorities in general and Price in particular would look for him was in what amounted to their own back yard.

In Argentina, Oscar Medina had used his considerable influence to learn about the criminal warrant issued for Barnes and about the general assumption he had carried out the murders of two men he thought had killed his father. The information sent to police agencies throughout Latin America also described in generalities the fugitive's military background, principally to warn them about his considerable skill with weapons. Medina read the material, supplied to him by an old friend in the police establishment, and drew from it an even more favorable impression of the mysterious northerner.

"The man deserves a medal," he thought, unaware of the dozens of other men Barnes had dispatched in the course of his military and other activities. More than likely, though, Medina would have approved the slaughter had the various victims, drug criminals and such, been identified.

The flight Barnes made from Rio to New York, given his cramped coach seat, was tedious but uneventful and his false but excellent credentials got him through Customs without a whisper of suspicion. He rented an inconspicuous sedan at the airport and went immediately to a prearranged location on a nearby motel parking lot, where he was to retrieve his other bag from a man, he had been instructed, wearing the coveralls of a specific airline cargo employee. The man, large and ominous-looking, was there, leaning against the door of an old van, but the bag was not in sight. Barnes identified himself and gave his contact an envelope containing $2500, the final installment on an amount he had negotiated with a Brazilian agent.

"There's been a change in the deal," the man said gruffly. "The price is $10,000, payable up front."

"Where's my bag?" was his response.

The man was about to repeat the terms when a large fist smashed into his nose, breaking it and driving his head back against the van window hard enough to crack the glass. That blow was followed by a second one to his stomach and a knee to his groin that made the initial pain seem pleasant by comparison. He slumped to the ground and Barnes kicked his side, breaking several ribs, before he stooped down to confront the incapacitated hulk, who was groaning softly. "Where's my bag?' Barnes repeated. The man motioned weakly toward the van, where the bag, securely strapped with the binding and a lock Barnes had personally applied in Brazil, sat inconspicuously on the front seat. He recovered the bag and the $2500, leaving the battered man to his own devices, unaware his life had only been spared to avoid needless police attention. Barnes, meanwhile, annoyed by the inconvenience and the duplicity but otherwise unruffled, drove off the lot and headed for Chicago.

*

Chapter Eight

"This could be a big mistake," Jack McCurdy thought as he returned the phone to its cradle and leaned back in his office chair, "but what the hell." He had just arranged a meeting with a willing Sally Crapper, whose amorous nature and naked image had monopolized his thoughts since Bill Price suggested he see her again. Price knew McCurdy had cheated on his wife, and he knew she had discovered the affair with Sally and put him on a short tether with the warning any further contact with the woman would lead directly to divorce court. But Price also knew Sally Crapper was the only surviving relative of Toby Barnes and that McCurdy might be able to penetrate, at least to some extent, the probable communications that took place between the two. He had ask McCurdy to meet secretly with Sally Crapper for lunch or dinner, extract what information he could and let it go at that, knowing, of course, that his good friend was not sufficiently disciplined to carry out the request. He also knew the kind of information he wanted was more likely to result from their sexual union than from casual conversation at lunch. The trick, of course, was to keep Missy McCurdy in the dark, a feat Jack had not accomplished in the past.

Jack understood his intentions toward Sally were at least dishonorable as far as his wife was concerned, but his rampant horniness stilled any concern he had in that regard. He loved his wife, knew Price was using their friendship for his own devious ends, but recognized in an attractive, personable and passionate woman the chance to exorcize what he presumed was a mid-life crisis. Or did he just want to get laid? McCurdy didn't know, but he felt an undercurrent of excitement as he retrieved his phone and called The Bristol for lunch reservations on the following day. He also called The Palms Motel and reserved a room, confident from his earlier conversation with Sally that their intentions were erotically mutual. As he completed the arrangements and leaned back in his creaky desk chair, he found himself humming as some kind of sly, little joke, "I'm In The Mood For Love."

Across town in an office scaled to accommodate his large size, Frank Tingle had also been on the phone. His new client, Sonny Spivak, had put him in contact with Sally Crapper, suggesting they get acquainted against the time he would use them as intermediaries in his communications with one of his clients. Tingle knew that client was Toby Barnes, a cold fact he had learned from his long-time friend and former police colleague, Bill Price. With total disregard for ethical considerations, the private detective -- who owed a serious debt of gratitude to Price - decided that obligation was more important than his responsibility to Spivak, a man whose moral standards failed to meet his rather complicated requirements. Tingle would pass on to Price anything he learned about Barnes, a devious but effective arrangement that would equalize to some extent the contest between the wealthy fugitive and the resource-starved cop.

"I'll be in the city tomorrow," Sally Crapper told Tingle during the phone conversation, and they agreed to meet at his office about mid-morning before her lunch with McCurdy. Spivak had explained that the private detective would assume a role in her communications with Toby Barnes, but beyond that she knew nothing about this rotund personality.

At their first meeting, Sally had the immediate impression Frank Tingle wore his great weight with grace and agility. He had emerged from his inner office to greet her near his secretary's desk and then escorted her back into his vast private space with close but not excessive attention. "He's a smooth operator," she thought as he adjusted her chair until she was comfortably seated and then returned to his own space behind a desk abundantly proportioned to the office and its substantial occupant. She didn't know at the time that Tingle had a reputation for romantic alliances with a long series of women, a reputation based heavily on rumors his sexual equipment was commensurate in size with his general proportions. There were those, naturally, who suspected the rumors had originated with him.

But it was Tingle's natural ease with women and his courtly manner that attracted her, although not in the physical way she responded to McCurdy. This attraction was mutual, based in Tingle's case on what he judged to be her apparent intelligence and good humor. They arrived at these mutually favorable opinions of one another despite an opaque conversation in which they both disclosed little of what they actually knew about their new association. She said nothing about Toby Barnes and alluded only in general terms to a vague arrangement in which she would pass information through him to the lawyer, Spivak. For his part, Tingle portrayed himself as a channel of communication and nothing more. "I'm a little like your own private phone company," he said, aware his duplicity could have a damaging effect on this pleasant woman as well as on the attorney he privately called "The Snake." He would have preferred that circumstances were otherwise, but he had long since decided not to complicate his life with efforts to fix the unfixable. "You tell me what to pass on to Spivak, and I'll see he gets it as soon as possible," Tingle added with a suggestion all their communications remain verbal. "No paper or computer trail," he advised.

"That makes sense," she replied, as they concluded the meeting and he escorted her out of his office, shook her small hand gently with both of his large ones and then gave her his business card with a private phone number on it. "Call me any time of the day or night," he said. She glanced at the card, thanked him and left, bound for The Bristol Bar and Grill.

"Nice woman," Tingle commented to Lily Smith, his secretary, as he passed her desk on his way to his office.

"I have no way of knowing," she replied, busy with the month's billing and other matters that made the business run.

McCurdy had at least been honest with Sally Crapper, explaining his marital circumstances as the reason for his inability to spend the night with her. It was one of those rare occasions when he had anticipated and done something to prevent what could have become a sticky situation. He had also stowed a clean shirt in the trunk of his car, recalling that a lipstick smudge on his collar had tipped his wife to the original indiscretion. McCurdy recognized his improvement in this sneaky business but still wondered if he could muster the presence to fool his perceptive spouse. More characteristically, though, he deferred the problem to another time, and hurried from his suburban office to downtown, where The Bristol provided an environment completely apart from his domestic life. He arrived only minutes ahead of Sally, who was early, and they took a secluded booth to begin what he hoped would be a long and pleasant afternoon.

"You're lookin' good," he said, honestly enough but without the polished charm of Frank Tingle, as they settled into their seats.

"You don't look bad, yourself," she replied, aware his rough social edges corresponded with a sturdy presence to create an effect she found not only attractive but sexually compelling. Sally, too, had recollections of their original union and was full of anticipation for the afternoon.

"How was your drive up from Clarendon?" he inquired, mostly to begin a conversation that would over the entire lunch reveal nothing to him, including her recent meeting with Frank Tingle. McCurdy was foolish in some things, but he was no fool. He hadn't been particularly optimistic about his ability to extract useful information from Sally, and had certain reservations about doing it in the first place. The whole thing seemed ungentlemanly to him, given what he really wanted from the woman. He also understood she was no fool, and was unlikely to divulge anything she didn't want him to know. In any event, he lost interest in the issue half way through their lunch when she presented him with a small, flat box, neatly wrapped in white gift paper with a matching silk ribbon and bow. He took the present and wondered, momentarily, if he should unwrap it then or wait until they had finished their meal.

"Open it now," she instructed, sensing his quandary.

McCurdy fumbled with the tightly bound ribbon, but soon managed to remove the paper and open the box. Inside, he found a pair of women's silk underpants with lace trim. There was also the scent of a delicate cologne, which he realized as he looked at the garment and slowly recognized its implication.

"I had intended to wear those today," she said to make absolutely certain he understood the message.

Later that afternoon, he awoke from a short nap, more than grateful his long sexual famine had ended. His wife had denied him her bodily premises when she learned about the earlier affair and had been rather indefinite about the duration of that situation. "I may be creating a new problem for myself," he thought, putting a hand gently on Sally's nicely formed bare buttocks as she slept next to him on her stomach, "but I've solved an old one." He had found a partner capable of multiple orgasms and one willing to extend services not available to him in his marital bed. The experience had changed him in some fundamental way, although he was unaware of it at the time.

Price had not told McCurdy about Frank Tingle because there was an unspoken understanding the arrangement was entirely confidential. Tingle's actions were at least unethical and, possibly, illegal, which implied that Spivak, should he discover the duplicity, might sue the private detective into bankruptcy and beyond. There was also the further possibility the lawyer -- given his ties to the local mob -- might try to extract some more primitive form of revenge, a possibility that Price considered but one that did not trouble Tingle. He had little fear of anything other than the loss of good times.

Price was honor-bound -- even though the word "honor" never saw use in his spoken vocabulary -- to keep the matter to himself, and was confident McCurdy would have understood his motive. He not only would have understood the motive, Price suspected, but would not have given it a second thought. McCurdy had a few character flaws, but the inclination to be offended by petty stuff was not part of his make-up, his friend knew.

The inability to disguise his guilt, however, was an ingrained part of the man, which was displayed that evening when he returned home and his wife, Missy, knew almost immediately he had broken his promise of fidelity. The first clue was the fresh shirt he wore. He left that morning in a solid white one and returned home in something with stripes. "He must think I'm an idiot," she thought before calling him to account.

At first, McCurdy vehemently denied her accusations, but soon broke down under a withering verbal assault from this small but assertive woman. He confessed everything, said he was genuinely sorry, which wasn't entirely true, and asked for still another chance. "I love you," he said, which was true enough, "and don't want us to divorce." She had warned him earlier that divorce would be the inevitable result of another infidelity.

"I'm not about to divorce you, miserable creature that you are," she said to his complete surprise. "I've given the matter a lot of thought, and come to the conclusion you can't afford a divorce. That means I can't afford one." She went on to explain their children needed a father, even "a weak-kneed cheat," and she had no interest in going to work to supplement the meager alimony and child support he could provide. Given those circumstances, she went on, she had decided to maintain the marriage, only on entirely different terms. "I decided," she told him, "that if you can have a lover, so can I."

"You're kidding," he said, knowing it wasn't a joke.

"Yeah," she replied. "You wish." She then explained she had already taken a lover and she would retain him or get another at her pleasure.

"Who is the son-of-a-bitch?" McCurdy demanded, forgetting for the moment he wasn't in the best bargaining position for that information or anything else.

"It's none of your damn business and I wouldn't tell you, anyway, because you carry a gun," Missy said. "But I will say he's dumb as a brick, has a cute little ass and may be the world's best lover." She concluded the conversation on that note and left him to ponder the consequences of recent events. Despite those events, she still loved her husband and didn't want a divorce for that reason as well as the practical grounds she had outlined for him. But she was equally determined not to be the only one in their marriage not having fun.

For his part, Jack McCurdy had a stressful evening until he realized his immediate problem might have been solved. As he struggled to get comfortable on the well-worn couch, it occurred to him the threat of divorce had been lifted and he had been reunited with Sally Crapper. "That's not all bad," he thought, thinking as usual about the immediate situation and ignoring the long-term possibilities. He wasn't sure about Missy's mysterious lover, but eventually came to the conclusion that fair was fair. If he could do it, so could she.

Missy had not told Jack the complete truth. She had, indeed, had something of an affair, but her partner was neither dumb nor the world's best lover. And his ass was nothing special. The man was her middle-aged gynecologist, and they had come together when, during a regular examination, she had confessed her husband's indiscretion to the sympathetic doctor. One thing led to another and they did the deed in his examining room one evening when she was supposed to have been at a PTA meeting and his staff was gone for the day. She developed a new appreciation for his stirrups on that occasion, but neither of them was thrilled with the result and mutually decided to reinstate their old doctor-patient relationship. Undaunted, Missy figured she would do better the next time.

Sally Crapper, meanwhile, had returned to her small, neat home in Clarendon, where she phoned Frank Tingle on the evening the McCurdys reached their new marital compact. The two events were mostly unrelated, but Tingle was instructed to ask Spivak to handle a legal matter for Barnes and to advise Sally when it had been accomplished. There was something about the message, Price noticed when it was passed on to him, that suggested the fugitive was somewhere in the United States and not, as he had expected, in some Latin American wilderness. Sally had alluded to an unspecified land deal -- one that was obviously within the national boundaries -- and Price wondered if Barnes had decided to double back on his own trail. Or was it just some kind of investment or other business that had nothing to do with any intention to settle down?

He didn't know, but he did know Barnes had used a Chicago real estate firm to assemble land parcels that eventually made up the Ozark ranch. And he knew a woman, one of the company's officers, had not only represented Barnes on those transactions, but had accompanied him through his various reincarnations and from one clandestine place to another. "It's a long shot," he thought, "but it's worth a try." He had decided to reexamine the real estate firm against the possibility Barnes had commenced further dealings with the organization, assuming his trackers had moved on to other things. As it turned out, the decision revealed a good deal more than he had expected. He learned the woman, Isabella Constable, had been reinstated to her former position, and he suspected Barnes was not out of her life.

The combination of information that Tingle supplied to Price and his own conjecture, based on experience and instinct, probably would have led to the capture of Barnes in Chicago had it not been for an unusual turn of events. Price had alerted the federal authorities, who quickly identified Isabella's new apartment on the near north side and put it under surveillance. But Barnes never reached Chicago, at least on that particular occasion. Barely away from the New York airport in his inconspicuous rental car, he received an emergency cell phone call that sent him in an entirely different and unexpected direction.

Barnes had established a variety of circuitous communications means for those he considered important for both personal and business reasons. There were various channels through which messages could be dispatched to him, but all quickly funneled into a single call on the cell phone attached to his belt. The call he received as he left the New York area was from a man with a heavy Latin American accent.

"Is this Mr. Cherbic?" he inquired.

"Who is this and what do you want?"

"I am an old friend of Oscar Medina," the man said, "and he is in trouble." The caller went on to explain that Medina was a virtual prisoner in his own home, held captive by a distant relative who had laid claim to the estate based on an allegation the elderly owner was no longer capable of handling his own affairs. That allegation, backed by false statements from cleverly devised fictional sources, kept the authorities from intervening on Medina's behalf, and made it possible for the claimant to force his way into control of the ranch at the head of a small group of hired thugs. The resourceful old man, though, had managed with the aid of his faithful driver to sneak a message out to a friend with instructions on how to contact the one person he thought might help him. He identified the person as "Mr. Cherbic," but now knew from official reports he had seen that his real name was Toby Barnes.

The fact the caller had access to his emergency phone line told Barnes there was some substance to the story, but he was non-committal in his reply to the man. "I'll look into the matter," he said.

*

Chapter Nine

Bill Price's caseload was heavier than one might expect, given the amount of time and effort he spent on the Moretti and Quinn murders and consequent search for the elusive Toby Barnes. But an almost predictable number of homicides were a fact of city life and Price – who was called on to investigate his share – originally considered these killings a form of job security. He had, in fact, modified that judgment somewhat in recent years as government budgets and police manpower dwindled and he and the other detectives were expected to handle more work with fewer resources. Price, like his colleagues, grumbled about the situation. Unlike his colleagues, he had the means, accumulated through his own prudent investments and a substantial legacy from his murdered aunt, to retire. But the plain fact was that Price loved the work even more than he loved to grumble.

The intermittent leads in the search for Barnes left at least enough time for Price to investigate a growing number of cases, some with intricate links to others. This was apparent in the Moretti murder, where the victim's control of specific criminal activities in designated areas had suddenly collapsed with his death, and other gangs sought to replace his organization. The police originally feared the volatile situation would lead to open warfare among the criminal groups, an outcome that was forestalled by the rise to mob power of Jimbo

Moscony.

James J.J. Moscony had been boss of an organization that rivaled Moretti's gang, but both groups and others had partitioned the city in an agreement meant to avert the inevitable bloodshed and police intervention that resulted when there was a collision of their individual interests. That agreement had been nullified when Moretti took a .50 caliber bullet to his head, and Moscony – never short of ambition, greed and criminal determination – decided to expand his operations. That meant the elimination of certain competitors, which he accomplished within days of the Moretti murder with a couple of judicious murders of his own. He and his men killed a certain Horace "Dogface" Doyle and Rufus Bernstein, two other criminal bosses, and mollified their gangs with various pay-offs before they had an opportunity to think about retribution.

Relieved that gang warfare had not broken out but left with two corpses, the police were forced to investigate the matter and Price, given his assignment to the Moretti case, got the job. "The chance of closing this one," Price observed to his boss, Mike Dunston, "is about as remote as Pluto, the planet not the dog." Actually, the two policemen initially liked the new arrangement, aware Moscony was the smartest criminal in town and one that would likely maintain a tight lid on his various activities. There wasn't any chance crime would disappear, they knew, and it seemed prudent to have it supervised by someone whose essential viciousness was at least restrained by intelligence. They thought Moscony killed only out of business necessity and not for fun.

Jimbo Moscony's bull neck and powerfully compact body disguised his considerable native intelligence and had often led competitors to under-rate him, an error that had cost some of them money or power and a few others their lives. He was an essential brute, made that way, some said, by the hard nature of his childhood and the life that seemed pre-ordained for him by those early circumstances. His father was a drunk who disappeared from what might loosely be considered a household when he was a toddler, and his mother was a whore, more from preference than necessity. She was, in fact, a pretty good whore if the standard is based on income and nothing else. The woman provided for her son's basic needs, but left him largely unsupervised once he could attend to his own bodily functions and feed himself without adult assistance. Oddly, this circumstance – which might have produced emotional needs in others – made Jimbo extraordinarily resourceful and taught him early on that the world belonged to the strong and crafty, although he learned this lesson in an intuitive rather than an intellectual way.

Jimbo's surface manner was genial enough and he was often kind to children, women and small animals that didn't nip at his heels. He was generous to those who served him, mainly thugs and a few corrupt city officials, and relentlessly hard on his enemies. In short, he was a pretty typical criminal magnified several times by virtue of strength, intelligence and sufficient luck that sustained him through a rather dangerous youth without fatal result.

Price had known Jimbo in a marginal way for years and scorned him as he did all those of his kind, although not to the extent he disliked most of the others. Jimbo's attitude toward Price was almost the same. He hated all cops, but he hated Price less than the others for some indefinable reason he had not thought to examine. Their meeting as a result of the double murder investigation was, consequently, almost amiable.

"What's up?" Jimbo inquired, as Price, newly arrived at the mobster's saloon headquarters, approached the table where he sat with two tight-lipped men.

"I think you know," the detective replied.

"I know it's no social call," Jimbo observed, gesturing for Price to seat himself, which he did.

"Lose the goons," Price said, nodding toward the two men, who showed no offense at the unflattering reference. Moscony gave the matter a moment's thought and made his own nod to the subordinates, who got up and left the table as wordlessly as they had occupied it. "Anything else?" he inquired.

"I know you know I'm here as part of the Doyle and Bernstein murders, and you know I know you whacked those two throw-backs," Price began. "I also know there's not a chance we'll ever prove it, but the system says we have to investigate and that's what I'm doing." He paused for a moment and, as Jimbo chewed on an unlit cigar, then continued: "This would be a complete waste of time, both yours and mine, if it depended on getting anything on a couple of crimes that got you elected chairman of the local crime board. And I'm getting too old to waste time."

Price went on to say it was common knowledge at police headquarters that Moscony had consolidated control over organized criminal activities in the city, and had somehow accommodated the eastern crime bosses whose local interests were mostly in narcotics and gambling. He pointed out it was the first time since a gangland truce many years earlier that a single person had controlled criminal business in the entire city, and the new situation had possibilities for an understanding between Moscony and the police department.

"What does that mean?" the mob boss asked. He sensed there was a proposal of some kind pending and he was curious about its content.

Price told him a small group of high-ranking police officials had agreed to ease off on some of Moscony's less destructive but profitable rackets if he would use his influence and thugs to sharply reduce incidental crime in the city, everything from small-time street robberies and convenience store hold-ups to burglaries and vandalisms. The small-time hoodlums and delinquents, their reasoning went, were more likely to fear retribution from the mob than the police, and the mob was in a better position to control them.

"We'll let you peddle drugs, gamble and run your whore houses, as long as you do it in out-of-the-way places where it won't offend law-abiding citizens," Price told him.

Moscony thought for a moment and said: "I'm just a small businessman trying to survive a bad economy. But if I ran those kinds of rackets, I'd have to think about the proposal."

"How long?" Price asked, ignoring Moscony's thinly disguised attempt to suggest his businesses were legitimate.

"As long as it takes me to do the numbers," he replied, dropping the pretense and telling the detective directly the deal would depend on its profitability. He wanted to compare the prospects with and without the police department deal. "I'll get back to you in a couple of days."

The proposition Price made to the gangster was a complete fraud.

He had devised the scheme to penetrate Moscony's organization and gather sufficient evidence to prosecute the man for murder. Price had decided he preferred the old division of criminal territories where at least several gangs ran the various rackets and no single organization or mobster, particularly a smart one, gained too much power. The old way, Price had decided, wasn't perfect, but it had advantages as far as a detective force short of manpower and other resources was concerned. He had not only devised the plan himself, but had not bothered to inform his immediate boss, Dunston, let alone anyone else in the department's senior ranks.

Price knew Moscony was a good deal smarter than the average criminal and might see through the deception, but it was the man's intelligence he had counted on when he conceived the scheme. Moscony, he reasoned, had a strategic outlook, which had enabled him to capture control of the city's criminal enterprises, and he might well see the broad possibilities in the proposal. But Price had to make the concept seem genuine, and he did it with phony details, including something he passed off to Moscony as a petty crime monitoring program that would determine the effectiveness of the arrangement. He also conceived geographic boundaries, equally phony, for certain rackets – ones that separated street drug sales and whore houses from decent neighborhoods – to show the crime boss the department was serious about the plan. And then he waited for Moscony's response.

"What have I got to lose?" he thought, ignoring the gangster's vindictive reputation as well as the possibility his police superiors might seriously question his unauthorized and unorthodox methods. Had he thought about those possibilities, he probably would have concluded Moscony was too smart to murder a police officer, and his bosses, given his long and productive service record, would let him off with a rap on his sturdy knuckles.

"Are you nuts?" McCurdy asked rhetorically when Price told him what he had done. They were in The Bristol, ostensibly for lunch the next day and a discussion of the Barnes case.

"I didn't have many options," Price pointed out, "and I don't need two more unsolved murders on my back." Although McCurdy, as a suburban police detective, had nothing to do with the Doyle-Bernstein investigation, he was familiar with the city gangs from his time on the metropolitan force.

"I don't think suicide is the option I'd pick, no matter how few there were," he replied. "If Dunston gets wind of this, your aging ass will be on the street." With his wife, gaggle of children and insufficient income, McCurdy considered the prospect of self-induced unemployment comparable to suicide and more dangerous than Moscony's wrath. He forgot that Price had independent resources as well as sufficient confidence in his departmental record to render thought of dismissal as less than a remote possibility.

"Screw Dunston," Price said, only as rebuttal to McCurdy. He figured Dunston would only fire him if there were no other alternatives. And probably not even then. Price had saved Dunston's life years earlier and created a debt for his future boss that was both hard to repay or forget. He knew this reality, but never consciously used it for his own purposes. Price simply did what he did because he had a certain degree of tunnel vision where his work was concerned. He sought direct solutions to problems and often ignored or deferred the peripheral obstacles until later, unlike McCurdy who often ignored or deferred the problems.

Price used the opportunity of their meeting to tell McCurdy he didn't think Sally Crapper was likely to provide much in the way of useful information and there was no need to pursue the relationship. With a direct line to Sally through Frank Tingle, Price no longer needed the snippets of information she might inadvertently reveal to McCurdy on a shared mattress.

"Now you tell me," McCurdy said, actually relieved because he knew the woman was not about to tell him anything useful to the investigation. He told Price as much and also about his refurbished relationship with Sally and the confrontation with his wife.

"You are a complete nitwit," Price observed, somewhat relieved himself that McCurdy had blundered through the whole mess without landing in some divorce court. He assumed the marriage would eventually repair itself, which allowed him to soon forget the matter. For his part, McCurdy was pleased to once again have access to Sally and he wasn't curious about Price's sudden lack of interest in the woman. He simply assumed his friend had decided to seek evidence in more productive quarters, which was true enough.

They were part way through lunch when the annoying tinkle of Price's cell phone interrupted their conversation. "Yeah," he responded once he had retrieved the small instrument from his inside coat pocket, where he kept it to reserve belt space for his Glock .45 caliber auto pistol. Price listened carefully for a few minutes and his response revealed to McCurdy that Moscony, apparently angry, was on the other end of the line.

Usually cool and precise, even in anger, Moscony was really disturbed and made no effort to hide his discontent with Price. He had discovered the detective's lie through his sources at the police department. Essentially, he had learned that no one he could find knew anything about the arrangement Price had proposed and it took no great intellect to deduce the whole thing was a sham. His anger derived mainly from what he thought was an affront to his intelligence, which he thought worse than a physical assault on his person. He took pride in his mind, which had been his strongest weapon in a long criminal career.

Moscony outlined a short string of facts that strongly suggested Price had played him for a fool. "You're a god-damn con artist and not a very good one at that," the mobster said.

"So sue me," Price replied and hung up. He returned the phone to his coat pocket and looked at McCurdy, who understood the general drift of things. "That didn't sound too promising," he observed.

Price shrugged. "Back to the drawing board," he said.

The two men finished their meals, mostly in silence, before Price revealed to McCurdy his suspicion that Barnes was back in the United States and, possibly, in Chicago with "his girlfriend." He had no way of knowing how close he had come to the truth. He also didn't know the surveillance at Isabella's apartment would prove futile as Barnes, originally headed in her direction, changed plans at the last minute in response to Medina's desperate message.

As usual, Price paid the check for their lunches, and they left The Bristol bound for separate cars parked in opposite directions down the block from the restaurant. The street was strangely devoid of traffic, which was the reason Price noticed a large black sedan double-parked across from his automobile. The windows on the driver's side of the vehicle were down and he either heard or sensed an idling engine, both signs, he realized, of possible trouble.

The detective recognized the danger and timed a fall to the pavement behind a large steel mailbox as the sedan, tires screaming, pulled away from its parking spot and a hail of automatic gunfire from both windows shattered glass and punctured metal around him. Still shielded by the Post Office, Price drew his gun as he got to his feet in time to fire several shots at the car as it sped away. He knew there was little chance he would hit anything, but it was a response he was compelled to make.

Despite the dramatic and noisy nature of the assault, there wasn't a single witness other than Price to the event. Although random cars, some damaged by the barrage of bullets, were parked along the block, there were only a few vacant stores and lots in this deteriorating part of the old city. As Price gathered his thoughts and dusted himself off, he knew for certain Moscony had ordered his execution. He knew his assailants had meant to kill and not simply to warn him.

"I thought he was smarter than that," Price thought with some disappointment.

*

Chapter Ten

The bond that developed between Toby Barnes and Oscar Medina was extraordinary in every respect. They had been together for only a day, and there was more than 40 years difference in their ages. They came from vastly different backgrounds and cultures, although there were certain similarities in their personal value systems as well as their personalities. Both men were clever, resourceful and tended to elevate their convictions on important matters to the point of absolute truths. They were incredibly flexible in some respects and completely rigid in others, which had created problems for both of them at times and had something to do with their early appreciation of one another. There was also the almost inevitable conclusion that Barnes – whose father had died when he was only five – saw Medina as a paternal figure, and that Medina, in turn, saw Barnes as a replacement for his two dead sons. Some of the reasons for their early linkage are no doubt indefinable – given the complex nature of such things – but the attachment was apparent in Medina's choice of someone to call on for help. It also explained the rapid and complete response he got from Barnes. Medina had old and powerful friends, but he chose Barnes to extricate him from his predicament because he knew physical action and not political influence was his only salvation, and this new friend, he knew intuitively, was the one to provide it.

Barnes had calmly advised the caller who alerted him to Medina's situation that he would look into the matter. His measured response to the stranger was simply a precaution, something he called "prudent paranoia," a condition that had so far kept him alive and free. But he began immediately to check the information and to form a plan for the extrication of Medina from his captors, should that prove necessary. "This could be interesting," he told Diego, who had barely gotten settled with Maria in Costa Rica when Barnes called him from an airport near Cleveland. He found the opportunity to take aggressive action a strong refreshment, particularly in contrast to his recent efforts to elude capture by authorities from various jurisdictions.

"What can I do?" Diego asked.

Price told him to contact several of their old comrades – men who had been with them in the assault on the drug lord's jungle bastion – and seek support for a new, but easier, operation. He also specified the ones he wanted for the mission based on their specializations and the likelihood they had maintained their physical conditions over the many months since the destruction of Zee's stronghold. "Tell them," Barnes instructed Diego, "that it isn't yet definite, but I may well want them to move on a moment's notice." By move, he meant travel to a common destination, where they would assemble to receive more specific instructions, conduct drills and anything else necessary to carry out a plan that, knowing Barnes, was probably dangerous. But they also knew the compensation would be generous, both in monetary terms and in the kind of adventure these men sought out for reasons they barely understood.

Using only his cell phone as he drove west from New York, Barnes chartered a Gulfstream III to deliver him from the Cleveland area to a Central American destination. He had contacts in the region from both his Special Forces operations and, later, the independent little war that had made him a wealthy man. Among these people – some in legitimate enterprises and others on or outside the fringes of legality – was a man who had access to an intricate network of spy-like characters throughout Latin America. He was the one Barnes employed to determine Medina's true circumstances. His agents, too, had the ability to scout almost any area for various kinds of information and to provide weapons, vehicles or other things that might be difficult to bring in from outside the various frontiers. Barnes struck a deal with this man before he flew out of Ohio and three days later met him in a San Jose hotel for a preliminary report. Diego had joined Barnes from his home in the countryside and they soon learned from their source that the message from Medina had, if anything, understated his dilemma.

The agents in the Argentine had neither seen nor spoken to Medina directly, but had learned from ranch hands and a domestic the old man was held prisoner in his own home. They knew little about the legal grounds this distant relative, identified as Carlos Medina, had used to secure a claim to the property, but they were sure it had been supplemented by force, and that less than a dozen men, visibly armed, guarded the main house day and night. They were a surly bunch who made it possible for Carlos Medina to achieve complete control of the ranch, according to the old man's essentially faithful but thoroughly intimidated employees. This would not have been possible in earlier times when the estancia had been mainly worked by range-hardened gauchos, replaced through attrition over the years by lesser men.

Barnes listened carefully to the report, and then asked the man to secure information about guard posting schedules, if any, and the kinds of weaponry the men displayed. He also wanted to know about surrounding properties, area roads and if this Carlos Medina remained on the ranch continuously or came and went as part of a predictable routine. And he wanted telephotos, particularly ones that identified the interlopers, as well as details of the entire ranch landscape and, particularly, the main house. Barnes had spent a night there and knew something of the general layout, but he needed more specific information to construct the plan he was devising for the liberation of his friend.

Barnes was a man who knew the uses of money, but also recognized its limitations. He valued loyalty, straight-forwardness and a sense of honor more than mere wealth, but he knew how to use his great resources to achieve goals he thought important. It was that money, freely spent, that enabled him to gather the information needed to devise a plan in less than a week, and to assemble his small team in a rural Costa Rican staging area only days later. As it turned out, the final plan was quite simple and easily within the capacities of his thoroughly experience soldiers, who had seen far harder duty in much tougher environments.

Oscar Medina, meanwhile, had not done well in captivity. His distant relative – so distant Oscar had formerly been only vaguely aware of his existence – confined him to a small bedroom but had done him no direct physical harm. The confinement, however, combined with a sense of outrage and frustration had put the old man under a great deal of stress that had aggravated an existing heart condition. As a result, he collapsed two weeks after his imprisonment and was bedridden without medical attention at the time Barnes and his men, traveling separately, left Costa Rica for Argentina.

Barnes had gathered a great deal of intelligence on the ranch and the men who held it hostage, but he was unable to learn anything about Oscar Medina's personal condition. This informational vacuum gave him a sense of urgency compounded by the sure conviction the ranch had fallen into the hands of a ruthless scoundrel. These circumstances compelled him to muster his men outside Buenos Aires on the day of their arrival, and to prepare for an assault the following night to liberate his friend, assuming he was still alive, and his property.

The plan's simplicity made the early stages of its execution a forgone conclusion. A single helicopter ferried the team – Barnes, Martinez and four others – to a pasture far enough from the main house to avoid detection but close enough for these seasoned troopers to reach it on foot in less than half an hour. They made their approach in complete darkness, using night-vision goggles to find both the designated landing spot and a narrow lane that led to the sprawling structure Carlos Medina held with surprisingly few men. He had not prepared to defend the place against anyone more formidable than a few ranch hands loyal to the old man. And he had been lulled into complacency by the easy success of his take-over and the apparent compliance of those who worked the ranch.

There were only four guards, two stationed comfortably at positions in front of the house and the others at separate points in the back.

They were casual in their manners, some smoking occasional cigars or cigarettes, and some napping from time to time as the long night dragged on. It was apparent to Barnes from the reports he commissioned that these men were not professional soldiers, and that conclusion was confirmed when he and his small force took positions on the dark grounds not far from the house. Barnes had made no provisions for prisoners, which amounted to death sentences for the thugs guarding the place, most of them recruited from the small-time Buenos Aires underworld. They fell one by one, either garroted or their necks neatly sliced by men Barnes had chosen for this specialized work.

Once the outside areas had been secured, they entered the house from two sides – Barnes leading his small party through the main front door and Diego with the others through a back entrance – and commenced a racket meant to draw Carlos Medina and his remaining men out of the rooms where they slept. The noise had been devised to avoid the dangerous and time-consuming need to individually flush each man from his particular space. "Protect yourselves," Barnes had instructed his men, "but try not to destroy the house." He knew what concentrated automatic weapons fire could do to the elegant old structure and wanted to preserve it, if possible, for its elderly owner. He had also told them to take Carlos Medina alive if they could and to dispatch the others as promptly as possible. And they were to find Oscar Medina, who Barnes thought was somewhere on the premises.

The general plan mostly worked and eventually accomplished its primary objectives, but like most plans, particularly ones of a military nature, the final reality was somewhat different than the original concept. The noise did bring most of the felons out of their rooms, half dressed but armed, and Barnes and his men shot them dead with pistols and shotguns. One, however, was delayed by the apparent need to consummate his forced union with a young servant girl, a circumstance that only delayed his death by a matter of minutes. He had gotten out of bed, stark naked, and was sent to wherever bullying rapists go when Diego entered the room and put two slugs through his chest. He had fired three times, but one of the bullets took out a bedside lamp. "Pardon me," he said in Spanish to the young woman,

Who had drawn the bed sheets about her body and cowered against the headboard. "I'm here to help." There was both fear and disbelief in her eyes, which abated somewhat when he left the room to search other places.

Carlos Medina, who had hired surrogates to handle the physical side of the ranch take-over, survived the assault because he fled the master bedroom – which he had usurped from the ranch's true owner – for the temporary safety of a small linen closet down the hall. He was found cowering there when Barnes and his men conducted a room by room search of the premises, which also enabled them to find the failing Oscar Medina.

"I knew you would come," the old man said weakly when Barnes entered the room. "I just didn't know if you would come in time."

"I came as soon as I could," Barnes replied, taking a chair to Medina's bedside and seating himself. "How are you?"

"I think this business has finished me, but the thing you have done eases my mind more than you can know."

Barnes realized Medina was dying and would not suggest otherwise to him out of simple respect for his intelligence. They were, after all, quite similar in many respects. But he had one final gesture he could make for the old man. "I want you to make a decision for me," he said and motioned for one of his men to open the room's single door. That act revealed a trembling Carlos Medina who, Barnes later learned, was a small time swindler whose recent attempt to enter a larger game brought him to his present situation. His wrists were bound behind him and Diego Martinez held him roughly by the collar of his gaudy shirt. "What do you want me to do with this miserable thing?" Barnes inquired.

The older Medina peered across the room at the distant relative that had brought him so low, and took a few moments before he recognized his former captor. "Kill the pig," he said in a whisper to Barnes, once his recognition was certain. Later, as Barnes personally took him out onto the front lawn where the bodies of his men had been temporarily laid out on the damp grass, the condemned man inquired in Spanish: "Who are you?"

"Your worst enemy," Barnes replied in English, vaguely aware he had committed a cliché but eliminating the only witness with a single pistol shot to the back of his head. The former Special Forces sergeant then returned to the old man's room, but not before he instructed his men to borrow ranch equipment and neatly bury the bodies in a distant field. Barnes, if nothing else, was a tidy person.

As the men carried out those orders, Barnes sat vigil through the night over the old man who, wordless during that period, died quietly before daybreak. Then, over the next week, Barnes first arranged for his burial on a low rise within sight of the main house and, later, brought in a temporary manager – recruited by one of his many retainers – to run the ranch until a more permanent disposition of the property could be arranged. Eventually, the place was sold to a wealthy buyer with the stipulation it would be operated in perpetuity largely in its present form and under the Medina family name. There was no real legal guarantee that ensured those conditions, but the new owner had an honorable reputation and it was the best arrangement that could be made under the circumstances.

Barnes left Argentina once Medina's affairs were headed toward settlement, but his men, including Diego Martinez, had returned to their various home bases a day or so after the bodies were buried. Diego had learned only hours before Barnes called him to the task in Argentina that his wife, Maria, was with child. Neither he nor Maria could ignore that call from the man who had given them so much, but the prospect of parenthood changed their notions about the future. Diego – his wife insisted and he agreed – had to settle down to a more stable and less dangerous life, one that would at least give him a reasonable chance to accompany the child to adulthood. And once he learned of Maria's condition, Barnes, too, agreed with them. He offered to establish his friend in some kind of commercial enterprise, but Diego and Maria had already purchased an established farm in Costa Rica with money saved from his share in the spoils from the drug lord's treasure. Diego had also been paid generously for other services to Barnes, and was now a prosperous man by most standards. The two men parted with a handshake in Argentina, both aware their lives would now go in different directions.

The inevitable direction Barnes traveled from Argentina was toward the United States where he had business that needed attention. He had also missed Isabella in those fleeting intervals between the various actions that had engaged him in connection with the Medina affair. As he flew north on a swift, chartered jet, alone in the passenger compartment, thoughts of Isabella were more enduring and his anxiety to see her gained in intensity. But Barnes was a man not easily ruled by those kinds of things and he mentally arranged a schedule that was practical from both a geographical and an emotional point of view. He rode the chartered jet to Miami, where he rented and piloted a small twin-engine plane for the trip to Chicago and an intermediate stop along the way. That stop was interesting in its own right, but it provided him with a brilliant stroke of blind, unrealized luck. It delayed his arrival in Chicago by at least two days, which was almost exactly the amount of time since the federal authorities had dismantled the surveillance of Isabella's apartment. They had decided the stake-out was a futile waste of time and resources, and his eventual arrival on her doorstep went, despite his imposing presence, completely unnoticed.

Although the smaller plane Barnes rented in Miami had only half the cruising speed of the chartered jet that brought him north from Argentina, it had the capacity to land on small, remote strips that could not accommodate the swifter craft. The plane still managed a respectable air speed and gave Barnes the sense of personal control he preferred as a pilot rather than a passenger. Flying alone and with a single over-night stop, he arrived at the Ozark ranch shortly after dark, inconspicuously landing on the familiar, lighted runway. He quickly taxied to a small hangar where he and a man who met him parked the plane, out of sight, for the night.

*

Chapter Eleven

"I assume you know Jimbo Moscony bought the farm last night," McCurdy said in an early morning phone call to Price, who had only minutes before arrived at his office in the central police headquarters building. The news of Moscony's death had not yet made the newspapers but the first local radio and television broadcasts of the day led with the story.

"I heard," Price replied, thumbing through his morning mail, which was mostly junk with the possible exception of a single envelope that looked, unlike the others, as if it had not been part of a mass commercial distribution. The letter had been hand addressed with a ball point pen and had originated in Stockton, which told Price immediately he had received something from Sheriff Jesse Jones. The rural police officer had used a plain white envelope rather than his official stationery.

"Any chance Jimbo died of disappointment when he learned you were only screwing with him?" McCurdy asked. He knew, of course, that Moscony had seen through Price's little con game, but he didn't know the mob boss had tried to kill his friend. Price had kept that episode entirely to himself. He had not even told Diana Hornbeck who, he knew, could be trusted with the information but would have worried about him.

"He probably died of excessive ambition," Price said, opening the letter from the sheriff with a small pocketknife he kept for the purpose in his desk drawer.

McCurdy told Price the early newscasts had little information other than the revelation Moscony had been found dead in the back room of his saloon only a few hours earlier. There was the predictable assumption it had been a mob hit but that – like almost everything else connected with the case – was mainly conjecture. Later, it was revealed that Moscony had died from a single, close-range gunshot to the forehead, which meant he saw his killer face to face in the moments before his death. In all likelihood, the killer had wanted him to know who had done the job.

The envelope from Sheriff Jones contained a short, handwritten note – more of a scribble but legible enough – which Price read as McCurdy sustained most of their conversation. He talked mainly about the Moscony murder, speculating at length on the motive and how anyone managed to get close enough to carry it off. The late mobster had survived many attempts on his life and most of those who knew him or his reputation thought he was destined to die of old age. "If they can get to old Jimbo," McCurdy observed, "they can get to anyone." He hadn't yet learned that a lone killer had apparently conducted the execution with relative ease. There had been no hail of gunfire from a fast, black sedan, only a single shot from an anonymous avenger.

"I've got a short letter from the sheriff in Stockton," Price said, interrupting McCurdy's rambling discourse on the Moscony development. "He thinks our friend Barnes has been back in the Ozarks." The letter – written for some odd reason in lieu of a phone call – said a witness had seen a man with a striking resemblance to Jake Pritchard, also known as Toby Barnes, on the ranch, and later saw a plane fly away from the place the same day. The witness was a local tradesman, one of the few outsiders called to the property since its alleged sale when Pritchard left the area. The place, Jones wrote, was "more secure than the state penitentiary" and he had not yet met the new owner or owners, or even the manager. The few townspeople who did rare jobs there dealt only with a low-level employee who manned the main gate and paid them in cash. "It's a strange business and I thought it might interest you," the sheriff's letter concluded.

"What do you think it means?" McCurdy asked, distracted from the events related to Jimbo Moscony.

"I don't know, but there are a number of possibilities," Price said. "The most likely explanation is that the stranger and the plane have nothing to do with Toby Barnes. The man was seen from a distance, I understand, and he wasn't even seen near the plane." Price went on to suggest other possibilities, including one in which Barnes stopped by to wrap up details connected with sale of the place, and another in which the former Jake Pritchard had retained ownership through some clever manipulation of the sale process. "He has a girlfriend in the real estate business," Price recalled.

The sheriff's letter was full of implications, but evidence of a continued connection between Barnes and the Ozark ranch was too inconclusive to justify Price's presence in the area. Instead, he called the sheriff later that day and asked him to look further into the matter. He suggested local tax and other records might shed light on ranch ownership or, perhaps, indicate some effort to conceal that information.

"I wondered at the time how Barnes managed to get rid of that property so fast," Price said to McCurdy. "Deals of that size aren't usually made overnight."

"Beats me," his friend replied. "I've only bought one piece of property in my life and it has four bedrooms, five kids, bad plumbing and a terrific mortgage."

Actually, the ranch had been sold to a small group of investors who began to sell off its various assets well before Barnes stopped there on his flight from Miami to Chicago. Isabella had overseen the transaction and Barnes had recovered most but not all of his substantial investment in the property. The new owners had not bothered to even visit the ranch, let alone get to know anyone in the area. They had an agent whose main function was to sell everything, cattle and equipment first and finally the land and buildings. The brief stop-over Barnes made was to retrieve certain valuables he had hidden on the property, and he did it under a pretext that apparently satisfied the new owners and their agent, who met his plane and helped him roll it into the hangar that night. And while the suspicion that Barnes still owned the property – held to some extent by both Price and the sheriff-was wrong, his sighting in the Ozarks was accurate enough and told Price his man had probably not gone off to the ends of the earth.

"Well," McCurdy said at last, "let me know if anything turns up on Barnes or Moscony." He ended the phone conversation with references to both men, but it was the Moscony murder that captured his attention. Like other experienced police detectives in the area, he thought the man was bullet proof. He was the one smart and crafty enough, they thought, to live into old age. Later, McCurdy's surprise would be compounded when he learned the killer had been face to face with Moscony and dispatched him with a single pistol shot. There was something about the circumstance that seemed remotely familiar, although he could not at the time give it more tangible form. That would come later.

But later that morning, Price learned the federal authorities had lifted surveillance on Isabella's apartment. "Those dumb bastards," he thought, irked by the possibility Barnes had made a stopover at the Ozark ranch on his way to Chicago. He knew that was pure guesswork on his part, but it was guesswork based once again on his often reliable gut instinct and simple reason. There was, he figured, an obvious romantic attachment between Barnes and Isabella, who also had the useful ability to assemble large, complicated and creative real estate deals. Price had no way of knowing where the mysterious plane was headed at the time it left the ranch, but he assumed its eventual destination was Chicago if Barnes was the pilot. These educated guesses were right on the mark, but Price understood the federal investigators were not likely to reinstate the stakeout on Isabella's apartment based on nothing more than his hunch. He needed positive evidence or, at least, some other means to watch the woman whose movements would surely intersect with those of the fugitive.

Since there was little else he could do, Price's solution to the problem was to conduct his own surveillance with assistance from Jack McCurdy and an off-duty Chicago police officer recruited with help from a contact on the local force. He was confident McCurdy would welcome an opportunity to get away – provided the trip was subsidized- and there was little chance his wife would object under the new and more liberal terms of their marriage. Price would provide the subsidy with his own money, and both men would draw on unused vacation time from their respective departments.

The three men, working separate shifts for a week, would not provide 24 hour coverage, but they would be able to observe Isabella's apartment throughout the day and for most of the active nighttime hours. They had only to watch the front of the building with its formal pedestrian entrance and a driveway that provided access around back to the underground tenant's garage and a delivery platform.

Price made the proposal to McCurdy during an inevitable lunch at The Bristol, where they met only a day after the federal surveillance had been lifted. There was some urgency to the project, Price felt, and he needed McCurdy's help to carry it off. Although McCurdy was interested and quickly agreed to the proposal, he had something else on his mind. He had arrived at The Bristol ahead of Price and taken a temporary seat at the bar, where he learned from the bartender that a half dozen cars and other property had been shot up down the street from the restaurant, coincidentally, on the same day he and his friend had last lunched together. McCurdy realized the damage had been done in the area where Price had parked his car, not long after he had received that disgruntled call from Moscony.

"Did you know about the shoot-out down the street?" McCurdy asked Price once they had taken a booth and discussed the Chicago deal.

"Sounds familiar," Price replied. "What about it?"

"I seem to remember you were parked in that area," McCurdy said. He watched Price for some telltale expression, but there was none.

"My car is just fine and so am I," was the response.

"Yeah, but Moscony's not so good," McCurdy observed.

Price looked his friend directly in the eyes. "And what does a few damaged cars down the street to do with that rat, Moscony?"

McCurdy then spelled it out for Price who, he knew, had understood the implications all along. He also knew Price well enough to realize he would not have taken an attempt on his life lightly and would more than likely have settled the matter in his own direct way. "But how in hell could he get to Moscony so easily?" he wondered.

"You think I killed that felonious slob?" Price ventured at last.

"Maybe," McCurdy said, not bothered by the moral question but very curious about the manner in which the crime was done.

Price pointed out he was a police officer, bound by oath and other things to support the law. Homicide, he needlessly explained, was against the law, at least in most situations and places. The little preachment went on for several minutes, giving McCurdy time to realize Price was quietly amusing himself and had surely killed Moscony for both revenge and to prevent another attempt on his own life. "You're a strange piece of work," McCurdy said to Price, who shrugged.

Over the next few days as Price and McCurdy made arrangements for their Chicago trip, Sheriff Jones learned the ranch once owned by Toby Barnes had been sold. He was able to confirm identities of the new owners who, he also learned, were reselling the place piece by piece. The information told the astute lawman that Barnes had probably disposed of the ranch at a fire sale price – which explained the speed with which it was accomplished – and that the new owners were merely reaping the profit that had motivated them in the first place. Jones reported his findings and conclusions to Price – this time by phone – along with the opinion it had been Barnes who landed a plane at the ranch that night. Although he had only been seen at some distance, the description of the man – particularly his size and military bearing – was too specific to ignore. The sighting had been made the next morning in broad daylight and the witness was someone whose judgment and vision the sheriff trusted.

"Crap," Price said to McCurdy in still another phone call, "I hate mysteries." He went on to explain the dilemma created by the sheriff's news. Had Barnes still owned the ranch, his presence there would have been very likely as opposed to merely possible for a variety of other reasons. But Price had learned to respect the sheriff's opinions and was inclined to accept his belief it was, indeed, Barnes who had been seen at the ranch. On this rather frail evidence, he decided to conduct the Chicago stakeout, which he had almost cancelled. "What the hell," he rationalized to McCurdy, "we both need vacations."

Diana Hornbeck, when she learned about the Chicago trip, prevailed on Price to accompany them with the understanding she would be mostly left to her own devices while they conducted the surveillance. Price knew she was more than able to entertain herself, particularly in a city where she had begun her advertising career, and he elected for her sake to make reservations in a first class hotel rather than the cheap outlying motel that otherwise would have been his choice. The hotel, too, had the advantage of nearness to Isabella's apartment, which the two men came to appreciate later when the stakeout dragged on. Price had the further advantage of Diana's company during his off hours, and McCurdy, working different shifts, found the hotel bar comfortable and convenient. And the moonlighting Chicago police officer Price hired to work with them turned out an amiable, competent young man who needed additional income to finance his growing family. All these positive factors, however, were pretty well diminished by late in the week Price had allocated for the job. They had seen Isabella come and go, usually by cab and occasionally in her big, black SUV, but there had been no sign of the fugitive Barnes.

"This job is beginning to lose its charm," Price said to Diana, as he settled into bed next to her with two scotch nightcaps he had just poured. He gave her one and leaned back against several pillows, tired after five consecutive days observing the same building. "I probably know this woman's neighbors better than she does."

Diana had discussed the stakeout with Price every evening when he returned from the fruitless effort, and knew he was frustrated by their lack of resources. They were too few to follow Isabella when she left the apartment, and they were unable to watch the place 24 hours a day. They were also without electronic surveillance equipment and access to other monitoring tools available to large, metropolitan police organizations. But Diana had an idea, which she proposed to Price as they lay abed sipping their blended scotches.

She reasoned that Isabella's grocery deliveries – which were made on a regular basis and were part of the high-rise neighborhood culture- would reveal the presence of a second person in her apartment, particularly a large man with an appetite suitable to his size. Her idea was simply to identify the store that provided Isabella's food and monitor the delivery items, all accomplished with small bribes to the apartment doorman and the delivery driver. "If her grocery orders are too small to feed both of them," Diana suggested, "I'd call off the stakeout and have some fun."

Since observation of Isabella's apartment had produced no results, Price thought the plan was worth the small effort and expense needed to carry it out. He and Diana had become friendly with the Chicago police officer hired to assist in the stakeout, and Price assigned him the task of confronting the doorman and delivery driver under the assumption his familiarity with the city and its people would make the job a bit easier. He had also come to like the young man, who was endowed with what Price perceived as initiative and other qualities he valued.

The young officer, George Watson, told Price and Diana early in the week he was available to help them any time he was off-duty and his pregnant wife or two-year-old son didn't need him for one purpose or another. Watson had graduated the police academy several years earlier and had performed steady service in his relatively short time on the force. He had grown up in the city, attended its public schools and gone on to a small Roman Catholic college for little more than a year before his acceptance at the police institution. The young man was, Diana told Price, "easy to like," an assessment she made on the basis of his quiet, friendly manner.

Watson managed to carry out his assignment with relative ease, using 20 dollar bills to extract information from both the doorman – who identified a small grocery market that serviced many customers in the area – and a driver who made deliveries to the apartment building. That driver allowed Watson to inspect one of Isabella's grocery orders, which revealed almost instantly she was not dining alone. Aside from a substantial package of meats – neatly wrapped in heavy butcher's paper – and a case of Beck's, there was a wide variety of other foods that suggested the woman either had masculine company or was provisioning herself for some kind of natural disaster.

Price had warned Watson to avoid any situation that might put him into direct contact with Barnes, but the young officer had instincts of his own and sought to get more direct evidence of the fugitive's presence in Isabella's apartment. He used his purchased influence with the doorman to gain entrance to the building and to identify her specific unit, which was situated on one of the upper floors with an expensive view of Lake Michigan. An exact record of subsequent events was never revealed, but Price later assumed Watson must have made contact with Barnes, probably in an attempt to confront him, and was shot to death in the process. His body was found later the same day outside a nearby building. The killer had done what he could to divert attention from the real murder scene, which was more than likely in or near Isabella's apartment.

Price was in no position to investigate the matter or even to advise the local police of his involvement in Watson's death. Instead, he and his small party checked out of the hotel and went home, troubled by thoughts of what had happened and determined to make provisions for the young widow. Price had also made another determination. "I'm going to kill that son-of-a-bitch," he told McCurdy, who knew him well enough to know the threat was neither idle nor unlikely.

*

Chapter Twelve

Sally Crapper had not intended to get sexually involved with Frank Tingle, a man whose reputation for those kinds of involvements was as large as his personal size. She enjoyed his company at their first meeting, but had not sensed anything beyond a mild appreciation for his general manner and appearance. Tingle was a very large man – solidly fat, in fact – but he was also considered handsome by some and was very well turned out in expensively tailored clothes that showed him off to good advantage. And he knew it.

Sally understood that Tingle's sole purpose in her life was the transmission of messages she gave him from Toby Barnes to the lawyer, Sonny Spivak, a device meant to insulate the attorney from police scrutiny. But neither she nor Spivak knew Tingle owed a long-standing debt to Price and had decided to repay it by revealing everything he learned from her about Barnes to his former colleague on the police force. She didn't realize that revealing almost anything to Tingle was tantamount to a direct discussion with Bill Price.

Tingle was a complex personality, one who could lie with a clear conscience to a woman he liked and at the same time honor a debt he had accumulated many years earlier. He had been discharged from the police force for alleged offenses that involved large sums of money, and had only escaped prosecution for lack of absolute evidence and a courageous record that at one time had made him a decorated hero among his fellow officers. He was an accumulation of faults and virtues on a scale comparable to his physical size, none of which bothered him in the least.

Although Price suspected Tingle of improprieties when he served on the force and had stood by him during the difficult period following his discharge, he failed to realize the extent of the man's corruption. Tingle had taken money – mostly to shield established criminals and shady businessmen from apprehension and prosecution – and he had done it on a grand scale. He had even taken bribes from Moscony, Moretti and Quinn, among many others, on more than single occasions. Had Price known the complete story, he would have shunned Tingle for the scoundrel he no doubt was. But the big man was able to conceal the real nature of his long and profitable misuse of the public trust, and his success was due in some part to the simple fact he had no sense of guilt. He rationalized his behavior, mostly in jest and to himself, with the comforting thought he had never harmed a hair on the head of any woman, child or domesticated small animal. But he had gotten away with enough money to finance a lifestyle sufficiently extravagant to eventually arouse suspicions among his police superiors and to enable him to live quite comfortably in the early years before he made his detective agency a profitable enterprise.

Tingle, like Sally Crapper, had no prior intention of anything other than a business relationship between them, but the situation changed abruptly during their second meeting. Tingle had invited her to lunch and she had made the trip from Clarendon to the city late in the week her lover, Jack McCurdy, was in Chicago with Price. They met at Tingle's private club, where he had reserved a small, intimate dining room meant to preserve their business privacy. The room – which had a commodious couch against one wall – would before the lunch was over also preserve another kind of privacy.

They began the meeting with ordinary conversation that led eventually and surprisingly for both of them to stimulating intimacies which, in turn, culminated in a union that left their clothes strewn across the floor between the table where they had been seated and the couch. "Jesus, Frank," she said, using his given name for the first time as she lay, post climax, on his great belly, "you're a lively chap."

"My pleasure," he replied, noting their food was still on the table, mostly untouched. Their waiter had been alerted to the need for privacy by Tingle, who at the time meant only to have an undisturbed business discussion.

"Frank," she said again, gaining familiarity with his name, "you're quite the gymnast." Her reference was to the variety of positions he had traversed before concluding their union on his back.

"I'd probably be in the Olympics if there was equipment that could support my weight," he observed, but she resisted the image of Tingle doing giant swings around a slender metal bar.

They eventually dressed and reclaimed their lunches, but not before a long, relaxed conversation on the couch where Sally reclined, apparently comforted, on Frank's bare stomach. They spoke mostly about the business that had brought them together and Sally inadvertently alluded to Argentina as she fondled his large, limp member. Despite the distraction, he realized immediately she had accidentally told him more than she had intended about either the destination or location of her nephew.

"Why Argentina?" he inquired casually, his hand caressing her soft buttocks, partially as a gesture of intimacy but also to keep her from slipping off his mountainous bulk. The gesture and his general attitude were reassuring enough to elicit an answer from Sally, who was usually more circumspect, even with Jack McCurdy, in those matters she considered personal. The difference, perhaps, was that she knew McCurdy was a cop, but saw Frank Tingle as more of an ally in the effort to assist her nephew and only living relative. She went on to tell him that a friend, whose name she didn't mention, had business interests in the Pampas, assuming - correctly, as it turned out - that he knew where those storied grasslands were situated.

"That's ranch country," Tingle observed.

"That's the point," she replied before diverting the conversation to other matters, unaware she had supplied Tingle and before long Price with a solid clue to the fugitive's whereabouts. Price would not get that information until his return from Chicago, but it gave him a notion of where Barnes went following the killing at Isabella's apartment. And of particular importance, he knew the trail was fresh and that his quarry had committed an uncharacteristic blunder when he shot the young police officer. Price sensed that Barnes was losing control of the situation, although he understood the man was incredibly resourceful and was still a long way from his gun barrel.

Once again, Price employed the contacts available to his boss, chief of detectives Mike Dunston, to post an alert for Barnes in Argentina, particularly in the vast ranching areas outside Buenos Aires. The distance from the murder scene in Chicago and, perhaps, the availability of large properties made Argentina a reasonable destination for the fugitive, Price thought as he awaited new information from Tingle. He had no inkling the private investigator was physically involved with Sally Crapper and assumed he had gathered the information on Barnes in his capacity as the go-between that separated the aunt from the attorney. McCurdy, too, was ignorant of the new situation. He thought her more frequent trips to the city were on his account, unaware she had developed the ability to accommodate both her lovers, one in the afternoon and the other in the evening, on each visit. She had simply divided her multi-orgasmic capacity in two and found it was sufficient to satisfy both men. They were, in fact, flattered by her apparent desire to see them with such great frequency.

"That screwball Tingle has delivered the goods," Price told Diana one evening as they sat with their customary drinks in her front room. The descending sun was visible through the glass wall and they were seated next to each other on the couch. "He's not only confirmed that Barnes is in Argentina, but learned today he's nosing around some large ranch down there."

"The man gets around," she commented. "He was in Chicago last week and now he's down in the southern reaches of South America."

"You'd be down somewhere, too, if you'd killed a cop, even one in civilian clothes," Price observed, wondering to himself if his presence in the southern hemisphere would serve any practical purpose. He also thought about George Watson's wife and was developing a plan to make an anonymous contribution to supplement her widow's pension. He had not yet settled on a suitable amount or the means to distribute the money. And he had not mentioned to Diana or anyone else the personal responsibility he felt for the young officer's death, a sense of guilt that had increased his determination to find the killer. His earlier search for Barnes had been based mainly on a professional challenge and to a lesser extent the pursuit of justice, both purposes now replaced by a primordial impulse for revenge. He no longer sought to arrest the man he had once grudgingly admired, but to kill him in retaliation for the cold-blooded murder of the young cop.

Diana, too, felt significant remorse for the events in Chicago, but had no notion of Price's lethal determination to find the fugitive. She had learned a great deal about her lover and friend in the relatively short time they had been together, but there was also much she did not know about this intensely private man. She saw the murder of George Watson as a simple tragedy in which the only guilt was assigned to the man who shot him.

As a policeman, McCurdy hated the murder and the murderer of a fellow officer, but attached no blame to his friend. He knew Price had warned the young man to avoid contact with Barnes, and he also accepted the inherent risk in the work they had chosen. It was simply a bad break for the young man and his family, he felt, and the only rectification was to be found in capture of the criminal who carried out the killing.

"Is Barnes alone or with someone?" Diana asked. She had Diego Martinez, her first lover, in mind and was uncomfortable with the thought he might assume a certain amount of guilt by association with a known murderer.

"I think he's alone," Price said. "His woman friend was questioned by police and released, but they've kept her on a tight leash." He didn't disclose the source of this information, but it was apparent to Diana he was in close contact with events in Chicago as well as in South America.

"Any word on his Latin friend?" she ventured further, and he got the point.

"Your friend from the jungle?"

"Yes," she replied. Price told her Diego Martinez was not, apparently, anywhere near Chicago when the murder occurred, and was not involved in the two earlier killings attributed to Barnes. "The man's only offense is association with known scum and there's no law against it unless you're on parole," he said.

She found the information strangely comforting as she sipped her drink and watched the darkening sky beyond the trees that rimmed her deck. "I barely knew him at the time I knew him, and I know him even less now," she remarked, almost to herself, "but I care about the man." She assumed Price understood her feelings for Diego Martinez were not of a romantic nature.

"He probably saved your life," Price said. "That's justification enough for your concern." Actually, he had taken her virginity in a steamy tropical setting, but that was an ancient reality, Diana thought, that had no business in their modern world. Instead, she made a request of Price. "Will you do me a small favor?"

"How small?"

"Try not to kill him?" she replied, aware Diego's fortunes had apparently been closely tied to those of Barnes.

"I'll try," he said.

As night arrived and the two chatted in the darkness of Diana's living room, Frank Tingle and Sally Crapper met in a suite atop the Brighton Hotel where they planned to have drinks, dinner, sex and discuss the business that had brought her to the city, although not necessarily in that order. They confined their activities to the hotel under an agreement, proposed by Sally, to maintain their relationship on a confidential basis. Tingle – unaware she had spent the afternoon with McCurdy – thought she was motivated by simple prudence, given the nature of their business arrangement.

Unlike their first union, which had all the characteristics of a cattle stampede, this one was more leisurely. Tingle mixed cocktails and then they both casually removed their clothing, hanging or folding items neatly while they talked and until they were both quite naked. They then took seats next to each other on still another couch.

"To the evening," Tingle said, raising his large, elegant glass, frosted perfectly by the chilled liquid it contained, in a toast. Their glasses clinked as she noted her mountainous partner for the evening was solidly proportioned. She was pleased to recall he was no Jello-like, shimmering mass. And she further noted his large organ had already grown a great deal larger with anticipation.

"Good heavens," Sally remarked in recognition of his condition, which had been caused by her profound nakedness and a provocative pose she had unconsciously assumed in the pursuit of simple comfort. Tingle – tantalized by her full, inviting figure – was unaware she had spent a good part of the day unclothed, counting her time with McCurdy and two refreshing showers. They had intended to enjoy their first drinks and dispatch business conversation before dinner or anything else, but their decision to undress changed their order of priorities. They came together in a sudden rush, each struggling to dispose of the cocktail glasses – which wound up on the windowsill behind the couch – that had become extraneous to their new purpose.

"Wow," she was tempted to say but avoided the word for its blatant banality as they uncoupled. Instead, she smiled appreciatively to convey the same message. His satisfaction had already been expressed in the ages-old masculine manner.

Once again, Sally told Tingle more than she would have revealed under other circumstances as they lay together on the couch, gathering strength for another drink and the eventual meal that would be delivered to their hotel suite. A man of substantial appetites, Tingle anticipated the wines and rack of lamb he had ordered, but was also mindful of the instructions she gave him for transmission to Sonny Spivak as well as other comments that told him and subsequently Price the specific location of her nephew, Toby Barnes. "Son of a gun," he thought, suddenly aware he had hit the information jackpot. Under most circumstances, he would have been inclined to call Price at once with the revelation. But the prospect of a good dinner and another go at Sally took precedence over that inclination and he phoned Price the next morning.

Tingle was essentially a rat, but he was a gentlemanly rat and saw the evening and subsequent evenings with Sally to pleasant conclusions. He genuinely liked the woman, both physically and in other respects, and saw no contradiction in his blatant duplicity. One had nothing to do with the other, he would have thought had the matter occurred to him at all.

She, meanwhile, maintained her own deception – which was her relationship with Jack McCurdy – and they were both content in their individual ignorances.

*

Chapter Thirteen

Diana Hornbeck assumed her recollections of the time she spent with Diego Martinez and the small band of insurgents in that sweltering Central American jungle were immutable, an episode sufficiently dramatic to ensure she would remember it in fixed detail for the rest of her life. She held that notion for years and only learned otherwise when she tried to reassemble those events after discovery Diego had survived into manhood and was allied with the fugitive, Toby Barnes. She remembered specific sexual events, particularly the first time, but the dangerous encounters with government troops – invariably followed by wildly irregular retreats deeper into the tropical forest – had melded into something that was not at all clear.

Among the snatches of detailed recollection was the warm, sunny morning she left the modest embassy where her diplomat father was stationed for the town square to practice her Spanish among the shop keepers, pedestrians and others who captured her teenage fancy. She had come to feel at home in that earthy and seemingly timeless environment, and was neither surprised nor reluctant when a young man only a couple of years her senior initiated a conversation as she sat reading on a public bench across from the imposing church.

The young Diego Martinez – even then a rebel with a government price on his head – had been attracted to what he considered her arresting beauty and had only approached the girl to relieve his general loneliness. He had been fighting in the jungle for months, and had only ventured alone into town to gather a few supplies not usually available in the countryside. His leader – a guerilla in the early Chinese communist manner – had assigned him the task because his youth enabled him to blend into the town's general population more readily than the older rebels. At the time, Diego had not yet shaved, although he had shown on several occasions an aptitude for the murderous business that engaged the rebellious little band. He hated the government's army – responsible, he felt, for the rape of his sister and other wrongs to his family and village – but he was essentially a religious person who had little sympathy for the godless dogma of communism. He fought along side the Maoists because they were the only ones fighting the government. And because he had nowhere else to go.

Diana was immediately attracted to the slender young man, whose gentle manner disguised a history and inner toughness she would not have understood at the time. The knowledge he had taken savage revenge on his sister's rapist and killed another half dozen men in irregular combat would have been beyond her juvenile capacity to realize. She was, however, very responsive to his inquiries about the book she was reading and about the United States, once he discovered she was an American. He asked her about her impressions of his country and dozens of other politely personal things that engage the interest of mutually attracted strangers. They talked the morning away, both forgetting the time and what had originally brought them to the square.

Diego – whose intentions toward Diana were entirely respectful – had no suspicion of her true age. He knew she was young, of course, but thought she was closer to his own late teenage years. He also had not a clue to the intensity of her hormonal impulses or the recklessness of her adolescent nature, both of which brought them physically together early that afternoon in a secluded cemetery in low hills outside the town. The sheer rapture of the experience combined with their mutual inexperience in these matters led them to mistake sex for love, which is a common enough mistake, even among adults.

As a result, they were simply not inclined to separate at the time.

Under the circumstance, Diego – still unaware of Diana's age and family situation – asked her to return with him to the insurgent's camp, a difficult life, he explained, but one that would keep them together. She agreed, motivated by an impulsive sexuality that momentarily removed any thoughts about the effect her decision would have on her loving and essentially decent parents. She had finally experienced a physical relationship – something that had dominated her youthful imagination for some months – and she liked it.

He, too, wanted to sustain the situation, not only to preserve a mistaken notion of love but also to relieve the dangerous monotony of his daily life. He presumed he could protect her from that danger, although he had not really thought the matter through and it would soon prove to be far more difficult than he had imagined. He had also not thought about the tough, old survivor who commanded the rebels and had sent him to town for supplies.

"You bumbling fool," the commander screamed in Spanish, which was heard throughout the camp when he learned what Diego had done. The young couple stood before him as other rebels emerged from primitive lean-tos and other forms of contrived shelter to see what was going on. They gradually converged on the small opening in the forest – mostly out of curiosity and as a distraction from their hard lives – to see their leader confront Diego and Diana. "Just what in hell do you think you're doing?" the man raged. "Are you crazy?"

Diego stood mute as his superior, who had always treated him with tolerance, perhaps out of regard for his youth or respect for his natural abilities, shouted abuses at him. He pointed out the girl, Diana, was more dangerous to their enterprise than the army they fought. She would, he warned, attract increased trouble from the outside and create internal problems as the only woman in their small band. He slowly warmed to the rebuke, using it as a tool to demonstrate his authority, and was striking the air dramatically with his fist when a disturbance down a narrow trail leading to the clearing captured everyone's attention.

"Army troops," a man announced, almost breathless, as he burst into the opening and fell to his knees, exhausted by a long run from the point where their enemy had been seen. The rebels had not yet been detected, but they broke camp instinctively and within minutes had collected their weapons and meager gear for a trek further into the jungle that covered their irregular retreat. "Saved by the enemy," Diego told Diana, as he collected his things and led her away with the rest of his comrades.

Their leader promptly forgot about the young woman in their midst as he calculated tactics that would enable them to elude the nearby troops and find the simple provisions they needed for survival. The leader's dilemma was Diego's salvation, allowing him to remain with Diana away from the older man's attention until the problem was mainly solved by the passage of time. Over the next few days as they put distance between themselves and their enemy, Diana showed she was no liability. Strong and athletic for her age, she kept pace with the retreat, never complained and covered her gender in Diego's only change of clothes. Luckily, she had worn sturdy shoes when she left home.

The forced march lasted for the better part of a week, a period in which the bedraggled band traversed almost impenetrable tropical forests, low mountains, heavy thunderstorms, rushing streams and billowing swarms of nasty insects. The insurgents had fled soldiers they normally would have ambushed, but their ammunition and other supplies were too low to chance such an encounter. They needed time to regroup and rest, which is what they did once sufficient distance – or so they thought – had been put between them and government forces.

They came to rest finally in a small, upland forest where the vegetation was less dense and the air more refreshing than in the jungle. There was also access to fresh water and modest food supplies, which they mostly stole from the fields and groves of large plantations in the general area. As a result, their exhaustion was gradually replaced by newfound energies, which their leader meant to exploit with raids against the enemy to get weapons and ammunition.

Diego and Maria, however, found other uses for their renewed energies, which had little connection to the older man's Maoist objectives. Once rested, they commenced a continuous series of erotic collisions that soon taught them more of such matters than they had suspected. They sought privacy away from the group for these attachments, which showed not only modesty but removed them somewhat from danger when the rebels came under unexpected attack from a formation of soldiers who had stumbled on the encampment in the course of a routine patrol.

Diego had protected Diana to the best of his abilities throughout the long ordeal, both from the harsh terrain and elements as well as from his leader, who would surely have sought ransom had he known her father's identity. The young man had carried her across rampant streams, massaged her feet in the night after long marches through dense jungle and protected her from the other rebels who were mostly too tired to have bothered her in any event. And he placed her safety above his own one final time when the sound of nearby gunfire alerted them to an unexpected attack.

Diego gave Diana his vintage pistol and instructed her to flee in a direction away from the fighting and along a path he knew would lead eventually to a small village. He also knew his instructions were dangerous, but understood there was no better alternative. The government soldiers were under orders to take no prisoners and she would in all probability not have been given an opportunity to identify herself as the daughter of an American diplomat. She was reluctant to leave him, not out of love but fear of the unknown, until bullets began to fly in their direction. He kissed her goodbye, watched as she fled down the trail and then took up his old rifle, cradled it in his arms, and crawled toward the fight to avoid the miscellaneous bullets that whizzed over his head. It was the last they were to see of each other.

Thoroughly frightened by the suddenness of the onslaught and the recognition she could easily be killed, Diana spontaneously forgot Diego as her previously raging hormones were subdued by the prospect of imminent death. She ran down the forest path as fast as she could, her heart beating wildly and the gun clutched tightly by the grip in her right hand. She ran until the sound of gunfire was muffled by distance and she could run no more. Momentarily exhausted by the effort, she dropped to her knees and then slumped against a nearby tree, where she gradually regained her breath and composure.

"What now?" she wondered as the sound of footsteps down the trail telegraphed the arrival of someone. She quickly moved behind the tree that had supported her exhaustion but was not large enough to provide concealment from the lone government soldier who for some inexplicable reason had wandered in her direction. He carried an automatic weapon, held at the ready, and would surely have shot her had he not been looking at something on the other side of the trail. Instinctively, she raised the pistol, held it in both hands with her forefingers gripped around the trigger and fired, almost point blank, as he approached her. He turned his head, their gazes met as the bullet struck him in the chest and he fell instantly dead on the rough path. She would remember his youthful face and eyes widened by surprise for the rest of her life.

She shot the soldier, threw the gun into the forest and ran further away down the trail, but this time at a sustainable pace that soon put practical distance between herself and the small battle that could no longer be heard in the distance. She ran with the determination of a long distance runner, stopping only when necessary to regain breath and strength until she was miles from the man she had killed. Eventually, she collapsed from exhaustion and was found, barely conscious, by a villager and his young son who had been out to collect wood in the nearby forest.

She was taken to the village, given care by the solicitous wife and mother of the man and boy who found her and eventually recovered by the provincial police who knew she was missing and assumed she had been kidnapped by rebels. Only a couple of days following her last contact with Diego, she was home with her anguished parents who assumed they were at fault for their daughter's ordeal. She, meanwhile, had regained her composure and was not inclined to correct them in that regard. The exact truth, she knew, would not be to her advantage.

Diana was successful in maintaining the lie because those things she revealed were actually true. She told her parents and the authorities everything except the part about Diego and the soldier she had shot in her flight from the battle. Her description of the body and mind numbing treks through various kinds of wilderness, and the privations of the camps were direct from her recollections and completely believable, as were the accounts of the rebels and their dogmatic leader.

Diego, meanwhile, survived the skirmish along with everyone else on both sides with the exception of the lone government soldier shot to death by Diana. His body was discovered later and there was never a suitable government explanation for either his death or his presence so far from the actual hostilities. The survival of everyone else was nothing short of miraculous, considering the intensity of the gunfire, but the rebels were forced once again to retreat into the forest.

Diego remained with his comrades over the next few years, alternately ambushing small military contingents for the arms and other supplies they could acquire or falling back into the jungle fastnesses, which had become as familiar to them as their own grimy selves. Endowed with native intelligence and, eventually, a good deal of experience in his deadly occupation, Diego, by then grown to full manhood, assumed informal command of the group when the old Maoist was killed in a particularly desperate raid on an Army convoy. Afterward and as a result of the new leadership, the rebels grew less and less political and centered their efforts on simply revenge against the government and its police and military emissaries. They roamed the jungle with impunity, emerging only when it suited their deadly purpose, and on one fateful day, at least for Diego, they extracted Toby Barnes and his small Special Forces group from the drug lord's ambush.

Diana had no notion of Diego's fate and had assumed until she saw his photograph in the Stockton newspaper that he had perished in what she recalled as a deadly battle that had surely taken many lives. Although her recollection of events during that frantic period with the rebels were mostly jumbled, she recalled in specific detail not only the sexual interludes with Diego but his constant effort to protect her from one lethal threat after another. And she remembered the young man she shot, not thinking he might have shot her had he had the chance.

The realization that Diego still lived and might be in some danger as the result of his association with Toby Barnes led her one evening to reveal to Bill Price more about her time with the rebels than she had ever told anyone. "I shot a man to death in that crappy old jungle," she confessed, quietly and between sips of her drink as they sat once again on her couch and watched the sun go down. She described the event, recalling especially the look on the man's face as the bullet struck him, and went on to explain in greater detail the debt she owed Diego Martinez for his unfailing protection. She continued, however, to withhold everything of a sexual nature, not because she feared Price would misunderstand but more because it was simply too personal and no one else's business.

"I really don't know this person," she admitted, referring to Diego. "It was so long ago and we were so young." Diana thought for a moment and changed her mind. "But if you know the boy well enough, you know the man," she said.

"That's true enough," Price agreed, thinking, however, that a lot can happen to change someone between boy and manhood, particularly in a dangerous environment. He had promised Diana he would try not to kill Diego, but he knew the promise was entirely dependent on circumstances he could not control. "I hope her Latin lover stays away from Toby Barnes," he thought, aware but completely unconcerned that the young Diana had surely been laid more than once in that distant jungle. Price earned his living through recognition of clues, hints and various human subtleties and his girl friend's confession had confessed more than she realized at the time.

*

Chapter Fourteen

Toby Barnes knew Isabella's Chicago apartment was under surveillance, but managed to leave and return to the building unseen while Price and the others conducted their fruitless stakeout. He had simply concealed himself in the back of her big, black Navigator when she left and returned or sneaked out a little used ground level service entrance and walked to a rental car he had parked several blocks away. But he had not anticipated the off-duty police officer's intrusion into the building and the confrontation that cost the young man his life. Barnes had shot him at Isabella's doorway, unaware he was a cop and in an instantaneous reaction to what he thought was a threatening gesture. He sensed the man was about to pull a gun and reacted in a manner that had preserved his life through many precarious situations. Later, when he learned his victim was a policeman with a family, he had no regrets for the departed but planned to make some monetary provision for the widow. His principal aim at that point was survival, which enabled him to rationalize almost anything he did to achieve that objective.

Barnes left Chicago immediately after the shooting, allowing time only for removal of George Watson's body from Isabella's doorstep in an unsuccessful attempt to divert attention from her premises. He had wrapped the corpse in a blanket and carried it out of the building, using the service elevator and his customary exit. He deposited the body outside and took the incriminating blanket with him as he left to retrieve his rental car. There was no practical opportunity to dispose more effectively of the dead man, and he was, in fact, lucky not to have been seen with his suspicious-looking bundle.

Despite the effort, police investigators – once the remains of the dead officer were discovered – had little difficulty finding the place where he had been shot. They canvassed the buildings in the immediate area and discovered blood stains on the carpet outside Isabella's apartment. Luckily for her, there were no stains inside the place, which made her a person of interest in the case but not a suspect they could charge or hold. Meanwhile, she was entirely baffled by this turn of events. She had left Barnes at home to attend ordinary business affairs, and returned hours later to find him gone and police investigators rummaging untidily through her apartment and things. He had called her office on his cell phone as he drove away from Chicago, but she had been elsewhere and unavailable to receive the warning he tried to convey. Barnes would eventually contact her with an explanation of the affair, but the new developments had permanently severed their former relationship and he knew it. He thought she deserved more than an explanation, but there was little else he could provide under the circumstances.

By the time police discovered the bloodstained carpet, Barnes had reached the Cleveland area where he disposed of the rental car and chartered another Gulfstream for an extended flight. He had accelerated his original plan, but with one major variation. He had hoped to convince Isabella to join him, a prospect that had died on her doorstep with the young police officer. As the swift plane carried him south, alone in the spacious cabin and apart from the two pilots at the controls, he weighed his diminishing options and eventually decided to settle, at least for the foreseeable future, in South America. The plan was to put as much distance as he could between himself and the Chicago investigation, and to make it as difficult as possible for Bill Price, with his limited resources, to find him. He had long since identified Price, mainly through information supplied by Sonny Spivak, as his principal pursuer, but had not considered him a major problem.

The detective, Barnes thought, was just an ordinary city cop without the imagination or international reach to have any influence on his affairs. It was not the first time Price had been seriously misjudged by an adversary.

His final destination was South America, but Barnes meant to cover his trail through a series of intermediate travel measures. The chartered jet took him to Dallas where, in disguise once more, he boarded a commercial flight for Rio de Janeiro. On this flight, however, he flew in the first class section, aware his earlier trip north in the cramped tourist seat had more than likely called unnecessary attention to his rather remarkable size. In Rio, his contact had through prearrangements hired a driver and an inconspicuous sedan to take him to an interior city and to an outlying airport where a twin-engine turbo prop aircraft had been leased in the name of Juan Caldera. Barnes knew his Spanish was not likely to fool anyone fluent in the language, but the name might just deceive someone on his paper trail.

He rested for a night at that remote landing field and then, comfortably and finally at the controls of a plane that would transport him to his final destination, took off in a light rain at the break of day. He piloted the craft alone through foreign though not unfamiliar skies, his attention fully occupied by the task and diverted from the problems he would otherwise have been forced to consider. Strangely for a man of his intelligence, Barnes neither thought about nor feared death. He was essentially a fatalist who had faced death so often the experience had lost its edge. This quality had often been his advantage, enabling him to focus clearly on an objective without the encumbrance of deathly fear. His main weakness, however, was the compulsive need to maintain control, not in his personal relations with people but over the ambitious projects that had marked his achievements since boyhood. He had been mainly successful in that effort, at least until he shot George Watson. That single event had forced him into a series of improvisations unlike his carefully orchestrated alternate plans, and it had cost him a relationship that was more important than he had previously realized.

Barnes had been attracted to Isabella physically - which is usually or, at least, often the initial reason for romantic relationships - but it was her competence, independence and determination that held his interest once the novelty of her striking appearance had worn off. Those qualities enabled her to ride out the police investigation into the young officer's death, and to decide her life would be much easier without Toby Barnes. She knew she would miss him and the adventurous life he had shown her, but the prospect of living into old age without a prison record seemed even more attractive to this essentially practical woman.

She had been initially puzzled by the murder outside her door, but it was not long before she realized something of that nature had been inevitable. She had been through enough with Barnes to understand his activities – while wildly adventurous and hugely profitable – had a dangerous side. This realization and her close brush with prosecution in the murder case clinched her decision to distance herself from a man she still found attractive. "Perhaps," she thought after she had given the matter a good deal of thought, "we can still see each other on rare occasions." She thought for a moment longer and concluded: "Assuming, of course, he's still alive."

Almost as Isabella had that thought, Barnes leveled the plane out on the base leg of his approach to the Medina estancia landing strip and soon afterward touched down on what had become familiar ground. And there was a familiar face to greet him as he opened the cabin door and descended the steps, his long legs stiff from the extended flight in a confined space. Diego Martinez stood on the grass next to the paved runway, wearing a gaucho-style hat with a holstered pistol plainly visible on his broad leather belt. Barnes had prevailed on him for assistance in one final project before parenthood and his new life in Costa Rica separated them, probably forever.

The new owner of the Medina ranch with the honorable reputation was nothing more than a front for Barnes himself. He had with Isabella's help constructed a complicated ruse to hide his ownership of the property, which was necessary as a result of his foreign citizenship and fugitive status as well as a desire from his point of view to preserve the land in accordance with the wishes of his dead friend. He had called on Diego Martinez to serve much as he had done at the Ozark ranch, but also to establish a secure environment after the lawless episode that had resulted in Oscar Medina's death. He wanted those who worked the place to know they were safe, and he wanted to recruit tough new hands - gauchos, perhaps - capable of both handling the rough work and protecting the ranch.

"How are things here?" Barnes inquired as they walked together the short distance to a battered, old pickup truck for the drive to the main house.

"Under control," Diego replied, his Spanish accent noticeably thicker than when they last met. He had only arrived at the ranch a few days earlier with two former comrades, men who had been with him during his years in the jungle. Armed and courteous, they had spent the time providing reassurance to those at the ranch that things would be stable under the new ownership. Diego, too, had begun a close inspection of the spacious estate and an effort to identify those key individuals who made this large, complicated place function. The task was a difficult one, but it had served to divert his thoughts to some extent from his wife, Maria, and their forthcoming child.

"How is Maria?" Barnes asked once they had arrived at the house and he had greeted the domestic servants who gathered at the front door to meet him.

"Getting fat," Diego said, not without pride. Those who worked the ranch knew Barnes for the liberation of Oscar Medina from his captors and thought of him - at least the less educated among them - as some sort of mythical figure sent by God-knows-who to improve their communal lot. The others simply appreciated the effort he had made to rid the premises of bad men. Diego had been quick to realize the stature accorded Barnes and anyone associated with him by those at the estancia, and was using it as an instrument to accomplish the task he had undertaken.

Before the day was out, Barnes met almost everyone who worked the ranch, most of them at a large gathering arranged for that purpose and, over a traditional beef dinner that evening, listened carefully to Diego's early findings. "I've only scratched the surface," he said, reverting to his native Spanish, "but one thing seems certain. We need to identify someone who can run the day-to-day operations around here, and to give him the authority to do it." Diego essentially sought his own replacement, and Barnes understood he could not expect his trusted friend to remain very long away from his burgeoning wife. “Do you have anyone in mind?” he asked.

“There's one man, perhaps,” Diego said, explaining he had not yet had time to know him well enough. That man, Francisco Baldi, had grown up on the ranch, son of a gaucho who had worked there until his death many years earlier. Tall and spare in his mid-40s, Baldi seemed to have wide knowledge of the general operation and the respect of those who worked with him. He had the further advantage, Diego told Barnes, of a wife and two young children, which suggested stability to the expectant father. Both Barnes and Diego watched this prospect carefully over the next few weeks, evaluating everything from his work habits to temperament. They measured the attitudes of other employees toward him and snooped into his private life to make certain there were no dark, hidden secrets that might bear on his performance as operations manager of a reasonably large enterprise. And they thoroughly reviewed another half dozen candidates before they decided Baldi was their man.

Barnes offered him the job, which he accepted on the spot, and doubled his modest salary with the promise of an even bigger increase based on performance. Not given to extravagant language, Baldi thanked his benefactor and promised him his best efforts. He could neither express the full depth of his gratitude nor would Barnes have wanted to hear it, but he would soon find a way to repay his new employer for what he considered a singular and completely unexpected gift.

As Barnes set about to understand in detail the workings of his new project, he also kept track to the best of his limited ability on those who sought his capture or worse. He finally made contact with Isabella through a variety of indirect phone calls and learned the local authorities in Chicago presented him no immediate threat. He also apologized – something he rarely, if ever, did – for the mess he had brought to her doorstep, gave her his version of those events and wisely put off until later an attempt to renew their relationship. “Be careful,” were her final words as their phone conversation ended, not exactly a ringing endorsement of their personal situation, but not the terminal rebuke he almost expected.

Barnes had no way of knowing his lines of communication through the lawyer, Sonny Spivak, had been completely compromised by the relationship his amorous aunt, Sally Crapper, had blundered into with the devious private detective, Frank Tingle. The situation enabled Bill Price to lull Barnes into a sense of false security, which was not too difficult considering the fugitive's near contempt for the cop's limited resources and what he considered his parochial investigative skills. More important for Price, Barnes did not know his escape to Argentina had been detected and, as he worked to develop the ranch, plans between governments were made for his capture and extradition.

Through international police channels provided by his boss, chief of detectives Mike Dunston, Price had deceptively represented Barnes to the Argentine authorities not only as a fugitive but also a threat to their national security. In addition to the substantiated murder charges against Barnes, Price also implied the hunted man was probably a British agent who had fought with the English against Argentina in the 1982 Falklands war. He failed to mention Barnes was a teenager at that time, and the Argentine authorities didn't notice the contradiction his age might impose on that allegation.

In all probability, the suggestion Barnes was a British agent inspired more action on the part of Argentine authorities than the murder charges. Argentina had long claimed the Falkland Islands – which they call the Malvinas – and their invasion of that real estate and subsequent defeat by the British in a war of only six weeks duration was still a bitter memory. Price knew this reality and used it to get results that otherwise might have gone ungotten.

Whatever the reason, a substantial force of Argentine police arrived very early one morning outside the estancia's main entrance and commenced a disciplined deployment toward the main house. They would have caught Barnes, Diego and the two former rebels by surprise had they not been seen by Francisco Baldi, who was, as usual, up early and saw the advancing police from a window of the cottage where he and his family had been comfortably located when he assumed the new position. Baldi's cell phone call to Diego alerted the four men to their dilemma and gave them just enough time to escape the house, board the nearby aircraft and with Barnes at the controls fly off with the rising sun at their backs as the police converged on the runway. Luckily for Barnes and the others, the sheer distance between Baldi's cottage, near the ranch entrance, and the main house was a matter of some distance and the police had elected to mount their attack on foot to avoid, if possible, premature detection and what would surely have been a bloody gunfight. They had, instead, given Barnes the margin he needed to elude capture.

"How did that happen?" Diego, belted into a cockpit seat next to Barnes, inquired as the plane rose steadily toward cruising altitude.

"There's only one way," Barnes replied, his thoughts diverted momentarily from a hastily devised plan to escape the inevitable search for their plane, which, at least, was fully fueled and had sufficient range to take them to one of several remote air strips in various parts of the country. The cagey fugitive had identified these alternatives before his first visit to the Medina ranch. "That little rat lawyer, Spivak, must have made some arrangement with the cop, Price," Barnes continued. "There were only two other people who knew I was in Argentina, and I trust both of them as much as I trust you." His reference was to his aunt and to Isabella.

"What now?" Diego asked, almost anticipating the response. He had come to know this man very well, and strongly suspected he had either planned or would plan something that involved the attorney.

"I'll get you and the boys," meaning Diego and the two former rebels who dozed in the plane's passenger compartment, "to Brazil and the three of you can make it home from there," he advised. "Afterward, I'm going to the States to complete some unfinished business and then I plan to disappear into the global mists. This hemisphere has gotten entirely too hot for my temperate nature."

Diego, who fully realized the authorities were closing in on his patron, thought Barnes should go almost anywhere other than where he intended to go, but knew there was no chance of changing his mind. Given that certainty, he decided to see his friend through one final predicament. "I will go with you," he said as the steady hum of the two engines supplied a backdrop to thoughts of Maria and the impending birth of their child. Barnes made no attempt to persuade him otherwise, his mind occupied with more immediate concerns as well as the instinctive knowledge that Diego, like himself, was not persuadable in some matters.

*

Chapter Fifteen

"That slippery son-of-a-bitch did it again," Price complained to McCurdy in another early morning phone call from his office.

"Who's he killed this time?" McCurdy replied, assuming correctly the son-of-a-bitch was Toby Barnes but off the mark as far as the offense was concerned. He leaned back in his squeaky office chair, took a sip of hot, black coffee from a vending machine cup and waited for a fuller explanation.

"He and his little gang escaped an army of Argentine police who should have either put his monumental ass in jail or in some over-sized body bag," Price continued. "He's either the slickest or luckiest felon in the whole, goddamn history of crime, and he's beginning to piss me off."

"There, there," McCurdy said, amused by his friend's annoyance but curious to know about the latest developments in a case that was beginning to take on all the aspects of a career. Price went on to read to him from a report sent to his boss, Mike Dunston, from an Argentine colleague that described the events in general terms but glossed over the simple fact the attempted arrest failed as the result of a tactical error. The police had through excessive prudence given Barnes and his men time to board an airplane and fly off into the morning sky. The report was generalized and attributed no blame in the failed enterprise, but Price understood the job had been botched and that Barnes had once again slipped from his grasp. He had no way of knowing the man he sought with such single-minded doggedness was even then headed in his direction.

"We'll get him sooner or later," McCurdy said with little conviction and as a conversational bridge to a confession his attempt to extract information from Sally Crapper had been a complete failure. Price had not told him about his arrangement with Frank Tingle, who had managed to tap the fugitive's aunt like a maple tree in springtime. She had provided a slow but steady flow of information to Tingle that McCurdy – who lacked the private detective's finesse – had been unable to access. McCurdy, in fact, had even lost access to her general company, partly the result of his natural curiosity but also because he had not been content to keep the discovery of her other lover to himself.

Sally had aroused McCurdy's suspicion when on several occasions her afternoons with him had threatened to extend into the evenings she had scheduled with Frank Tingle. Her nervousness and poorly constructed excuses revealed to the detective that something was amiss, and one day he followed her to Tingle's hotel where all the elements in the mystery came clear. McCurdy – unwilling to share her services – confronted Sally with this discovery and she quietly told him to get lost, which he did with some later regrets. Still sipping his coffee, which had now cooled, he revealed these events to Price as a means of disclosing that Sally Crapper was not likely to provide much in the way of information about Toby Barnes.

"I didn't really expect much from her," Price lied, mostly to ease his friend's feelings, but now understood how Tingle had managed to pry so much useful information from the fugitive's aunt. "That fat man is a real piece of work," he thought.

Frank Tingle had no knowledge of the events in Argentina, but was quick to realize something had changed in the communications between Sally Crapper and Sonny Spivak. The slow but steady exchange between the two stopped abruptly, a circumstance Tingle reported to Price once he understood the circuit had been permanently rather than temporarily shut down. Price, of course, knew Barnes had fled the ranch and probably Argentina, but initially wondered why the line of communication between the aunt and the attorney had been broken. He eventually figured Barnes guessed the source of the leak based on a process of elimination. He realized there were only a few people who knew he was in Argentina, and drew inevitable conclusions from that knowledge. Price understood the general situation, but did not yet know Barnes had settled on Spivak as the principal source of his betrayal.

Spivak, meanwhile, was slow to understand his arrangement with Barnes had been terminated. He had an active law practice as well as a variety of other business interests - some of them legitimate - and usually spent his time flitting from one matter to another. He missed entirely the signal that should have told him something had gone wrong in his relations with Barnes, but he would not have been concerned even had he got that message. Spivak knew Barnes only as a former military man and had no clue to his lethal record. The lawyer had defended dozens of killers, alleged and known, but Barnes had killed more men by himself than the total accumulated by those on Spivak's murderous client list. Had he understood the true situation - which was unlikely given the fugitive's secretive nature - the usually cautious attorney would have left town on an extended vacation. As it was, he went about his crooked day-to-day business unaware the worst trouble of his life would shortly confront him.

"Frank," Sally Crapper said to her momentarily spent lover as they lay next to one another on the king size bed in his hotel suite, "I won't be coming to the city for a while."

"Anything wrong?" he inquired.

"No," she replied, "just an accumulation of things I haven't gotten done as a result of all these little trips to see you." The excuse was plausible, given the frequency of their meetings, but Tingle suspected there was some connection between the disruption of communications with Spivak and her decision to stay home.

"I could drive down to Clarendon to see you when I have free time," he offered, but she politely declined the proposal. "I'm crazy about our time together, but I have some business that needs attention," she explained. "I'll call you when things settle down, probably in about a week."

"I can live with that," Tingle said, gently restraining her as she attempted to get up and dress for the drive back to Clarendon. As he kissed her, she settled back into the bed. "Oh, what the hell," she thought as the big man began to do it again.

Tingle later recalled her reference to the week she would be indisposed, at least as far as he was concerned, and passed the information to Price who put two and two together and came up with a large question mark. There was the possibility the matter that needed her attention had something to do with her nephew, he speculated, but also realized there were countless other possible explanations. "She just might need a break from Frank Tingle," he thought.

Price was reluctant to reveal this conundrum to McCurdy, who remained ignorant of Tingle's role in the case, but discussed it at length with Diana, whose intuition told her Sally Crapper's business did have something to do with Toby Barnes. "I think it's likely the two will meet," she said as they had drinks that evening at the bar in The Bristol. "They've been in regular contact for reasons we don't understand, and whatever it is that ties them together – aside from their blood relationship – probably has more importance now the police are on his heels."

"Maybe," Price said, but realized the assumption Sally Crapper would soon connect with her nephew gave him the only immediate course of action that made sense. Diana's intuition was the basis for another stakeout, but this one outside the aunt's home in Clarendon. Price also intended to shadow the woman wherever she went, which meant the trail was more likely to take him or McCurdy to the super market or hairdresser than to Toby Barnes. He had decided he once again needed McCurdy's backup and local police assistance as well to carry out the plan.

Price knew the local police chief, Stan Blankenship, from the earliest stages of his investigation into the murders of Albert Moretti, born Albert Simmons, and Fred Quinn, who Barnes had shot in the mistaken notion they killed his father. The two veteran policemen – one from the city and the other from a small town – had certain values in common, and Price correctly assumed he could count on

Blankenship for whatever help he could provide with his modest resources. McCurdy, once again, drew on his substantial backlog of unused vacation time from his regular job to work the stakeout, partly as a favor to Price but mostly for his own amusement. The backlog had accumulated over the years he had been chronically unable to afford vacations.

Price personally underwrote the miscellaneous expenses related to the stakeout and provided a modest hourly wage for the single officer from the local force who, like McCurdy, did the work on his own time. There was the possibility Mike Dunston would have allocated departmental funds for the investigation, but time was short and Price was reluctant to seek money for something he saw as a long shot. But it was a shot he was willing to make because it was the only one available to him.

"Jack," he said to McCurdy when he sought his help, "I want you with me on this, but I'll personally kick your aging ass if you try to reconnect with that Clapper woman while we're on the job. Afterwards, I don't care."

"She's history," McCurdy replied. "I try not to make the same mistake twice." Price wasn't entirely impressed – knowing his friend was more than capable of doing exactly that – but assumed he could restrain himself at least for the week or less the stakeout would run. McCurdy's mistakes, he knew, were usually personal in nature, but he was an experienced, competent professional who could be trusted to carry out an assignment.

The Clarendon stakeout was more difficult than the one Price had conducted outside Isabella's Chicago apartment, mainly because the presence of strangers in a small town neighborhood was far more conspicuous than in a congested metropolitan environment. There was also the added possibility the two out-of-town policemen – both well known to Sally Crapper – might accidentally confront her in the course of some routine activity. For that reason, Price booked rooms at the Clarendon Holloway Inn, the only motel in the community and a place where the two men planned to spend most of their off duty hours. "I'd just as soon live in a cave," McCurdy complained to Price when he saw the aging place, but agreed there was no other practical alternative. Price, on the other hand, saw it as an opportunity to catch up on the reading he often deferred to more immediate demands – cleaning his guns or polishing his shoes, among others.

The Clarendon officer that chief Blankenship loaned to Price had never been on a stakeout, but he had effectively policed the community for some years and was chosen for his reliability and plain common sense. His principal problem on the stakeout was concealment because Sally Crapper knew him, just as she and most of the town's other citizens knew everyone on the local police force.

There was for Price another and more important consideration that related to the death of George Watson outside Isabella's apartment. He was not inclined to disclose those details to the Clarendon officer, but he didn't want a repetition of the Chicago tragedy. "This man can kill you a dozen different ways, and he's done all of them," Price told the officer, unaware the remark contained more truth than he knew. "He's big, strong, dangerous and I don't want you under any circumstance to approach him alone. Call me immediately at the motel if you see anything that looks remotely suspicious or even unusual." He peered directly into the officer's eyes. "Call me," he said, "if you see a strange dog in the neighborhood."

As Price assembled and instructed his small team in Clarendon, Barnes and Diego arrived in the city. They had made their way north across a number of international boundaries using false documents and various transportation modes, some prearranged and others devised at particular moments to avoid possible detection and capture. Barnes, distracted by thought, said little throughout the journey to Diego, who had entirely negative feelings about the whole enterprise. But he kept those feelings to himself, aware Barnes would neither explain his intentions nor change his course.

"This business will soon be over," Barnes said to Diego at last after they had parked their rental car, registered at a downtown hotel and gone to the small suite they would share for the night. "When I'm finished here, I plan to see my mother's sister in a nearby town, and then leave the country for good." He explained further he would charter a plane that would take Diego back to Costa Rica and then he would go separately to some place sufficiently distant and remote to ensure a more peaceful and stable life. Diego had meant to support his friend and benefactor, but he was left largely to himself over the evening and following day as Barnes made various telephone arrangements and left the hotel from time to time with only a general indication of when he would return. With patience that his hard life had forced into him, Diego passed the time cleaning his gun, napping or listlessly watching television he barely understood until Barnes finally returned and told him it was time to go.

"I think," Diego told Barnes, who was at the wheel as they drove south to Clarendon, "that you didn't need me for whatever it was you had to do."

"Probably not," Barnes replied with his usual candor, "but I knew I couldn't convince you otherwise and it's been good to have your company." He reached into his shirt pocket and retrieved a slip of paper, which he handed to Diego. "This is the information on the chartered plane, which will be waiting for you tomorrow morning," he said. "I'll take you to the airport, but you need to know what's going on in the event we get separated." Barnes had no inkling there would be a separation, but his survival until then had relied heavily on alternate plans and it was a habit he could not easily abandon. Diego had learned to appreciate these precautions, but wondered as they drove through the mid-western countryside toward Clarendon if it would be enough to see his mentor through to a new and safer life.

Barnes had called his aunt from the city and she expected his visit, but had not noticed the stakeout that had been carefully installed outside her modest home near the outskirts of town. Strangely enough, given their previous closeness, Jack McCurdy was parked at some distance down the block and next to a large vacant parcel of land where he was unlikely to arouse anyone's suspicions. He had a clear view of her house and powerful binoculars that enabled him to examine the area in great detail. He was also in periodic phone communication with Price, who had settled in at the Holloway Inn with Samuel Eliot Morison's two volumes on "The European Discovery of America" and an anchovy pizza that had been delivered to his room as the sun settled behind the motel parking lot where Barnes and Diego would soon arrive.

“I’ve been in cemeteries that were rowdier than this neighborhood,” McCurdy reported to Price an hour after he had taken up his position on the first shift. He was scheduled for relief later that night by the local police officer, who Price would in turn relieve in the early hours of the morning.

“You’ve been in that lady’s neighborhood before,” Price observed, setting his book aside and taking a slice of cold pizza from the flat cardboard box on the bed next to him. “Do you have a good view of the place?”

“Yeah,” McCurdy replied. “There’s a bright street lamp outside the house that lights up the driveway and front entrance. I can also tell when inside lights are turned on or off because the building next door is set back from the street and gives me a clear view of the side windows.” Price – who had selected the location for those particular advantages – had only asked the question to justify a routine phone call, and concluded their conversation with an equally unnecessary request. “Let me know if anything turns up,” he said.

“Why not,” McCurdy responded and then, alone once more, slowly settled into a thought process that inevitably recalled his more intimate moments with the woman he now spied upon. “Life is one strange mother,” he said quietly to himself as he fidgeted from time to time in the cramped car seat.

Not long after his conversation with McCurdy, Price set his book aside and gradually settled into a light sleep, fully clothed with the exception of the suit coat and tie he had removed some time earlier. As he slumbered peacefully, Toby Barnes and Diego Martinez arrived at the Holloway Inn and checked into separate rooms. The coincidence would have been remarkable had there been any other motels in town.

*

Chapter Sixteen

Bill Price learned of Sonny Spivak's murder from Frank Tingle, who phoned him with the news at the Holloway Inn shortly before the slumbering policeman was scheduled to relieve McCurdy on the stakeout. "I didn't like the guy," Tingle said, "but I never thought a bad personality was justification for homicide."

Price, barely awake, took some moments to digest the information as he looked at the bedside clock and then sat up with the full realization of what had happened. "When and where?" he inquired.

"They found him several hours ago in his apartment," Tingle replied. "There hasn't been time for a full examination of the body, but they think he drowned."

"Drowned?"

"Yeah," Tingle continued. "Somebody apparently stuck his head in the toilet and held it there until the poor sap cashed in. His hair was still damp when they found him." The body was discovered on the bathroom floor by the apartment manager, who had been called by Spivak's secretary when her boss failed to make several important business appointments the prior day. There had been no witnesses and no sounds anyone heard of a struggle, although, Tingle had learned, there was severe bruising on the back of the victim's neck. "I think it's clear someone with considerable strength held the poor bastard's head under water and pinned his arms down at the same time," the private detective observed. "That's no job for a weakling."

Price, now fully awake, had not yet sorted things out, but the nature of the murder not only suggested a killer with great strength but one with a score to settle. "I think Barnes has come home," he thought, but kept it to himself until a little later when he phoned McCurdy with the news. As he stood up and stepped out of his rumpled pants with the intention of showering, he thanked Tingle for the call and wondered for a moment where someone outside the police department had gotten the information so early. He knew better than to ask because he also knew the private detective never revealed his sources.

Price called McCurdy before he showered, not only to tell him about the Spivak murder but to issue the same warning he had given to the Clarendon officer. "Don't try to take him alone," he told his friend. "You know what happened in Chicago."

"Don't worry," McCurdy reassured him. "I plan to die in bed with clean, white sheets and with full insurance coverage. My long-suffering wife wouldn't have it any other way."

In the shower a little later, Price realized that Barnes might well be in or approaching Clarendon at that very moment, but had no notion the fugitive and his friend were actually in nearby rooms at the Holloway Inn. The man he had sought for so long was, in fact, wide awake despite the early hour. As a strong stream of hot water pelted Price's chest, Barnes sat at the plain desk in his room arranging legal papers he meant to provide his aunt. The principal purpose of the trip – other than to say a permanent goodbye – was to make financial provisions that would ensure her a comfortable life. As it was, Sally Crapper was modestly well off in a financial way, but her nephew, always one for backup plans, wanted to make certain she was secured against the uncertainties of life. He had earlier told Diego, who now slept soundly in his own room, that he would go alone to see his aunt and then return to pick him up for the trip to the airport. "I doubt I'll be gone more than an hour or two," he had said when they went to their separate rooms after check in at the motel.

Price had originally assumed Barnes would be traveling alone and that he would go directly to his aunt's home. There was no reason to believe he had any other contacts in Clarendon or that he would spend any more time in the town than necessary to see Sally Crapper for the reason or reasons that had brought him back to the place where he had spent the first five years of his life. Price assumed the nature of the business that connected the nephew and the aunt was more complicated than the reality. He thought, perhaps, it had something to do with the far-flung and tangled affairs of the fugitive, which would have explained the regular communications they had maintained through Sonny Spivak and Frank Tingle. He would have been surprised to learn that Barnes had sustained the contact for certain practical reasons, but mostly because Sally Crapper was his dead mother's sister and his only living relative. They were kin.

As Price emerged from the shower, he recalled that the Holloway Inn was the only motel in town. "Is it possible that Barnes plans to stay here?" he thought. "Could he have made a reservation?" He finished drying himself, pulled on a fresh pair of boxer shorts from his small travel bag, and called the front desk, where a sleepy clerk failed to understand his question. It was not yet four in the morning.

"I'm a police officer associated with your local police chief, and I want to know if you have any single reservations for today or tomorrow?" he asked again. The question would have been ridiculous at most motels, particularly busy ones, but Price had seen the sparsely populated parking lot at the Holloway Inn and new the booking would be light.

"I'm not sure I can give out that information," the clerk, a young man, judging by his voice, said with absolute uncertainty.

"You can call Chief Blankenship, but do it now," Price said with authority. The clerk, apparently convinced, mumbled something barely coherent but meant to explain he needed a moment to examine the registration book. Price could hear him fumbling with something, presumably that book, and shuffling through pages for a few moments before he said: "We have eight reservations for tomorrow night, five singles and three couples." The clerk recited the names and addresses for Price, who was unable to discover anything useful from the information. Barnes, he knew, was not likely to use his real name and would certainly have fabricated an address.

“Will you be around for the next few nights?” Price inquired.

“I’m here six nights a week and won’t be off until Saturday,” was the response. The clerk’s interest had been aroused by the prospect of something that might relieve the monotony of his long, lonely nighttime vigils. “Anything I can do?” he asked, an element of expectancy in his voice.

“As a matter of fact, there is,” Price said. “You can alert me or Mr. McCurdy in room 210 if a man who fits this description checks into the motel.” He then described in significant detail Toby Barnes, stressing his singular height and carriage as his most distinguishing features. There was silence at the other end of the phone line. “Are you still there?” Price wanted to know.

“That sounds like Mr. Bingham in room 106,” the clerk replied at last. “He checked in late yesterday afternoon, not long after I came to work.”

“Bingo,” Price thought as the clerk recalled and revealed that Mr. Bingham, although he had a room to himself, had not been alone. He had been with another man, who had checked into room 108. The other man, Price soon learned, fit the description of the mysterious figure who was not only closely associated with Toby Barnes but had been Diana’s protector in that long-ago jungle.

Price instructed the clerk to remain at the front desk, particularly over the next hour or two. “Don’t do anything unusual and don’t call anyone,” he ordered before he hung up and called McCurdy on his cell phone. “I think we’ve got the son-of-a-bitch,” he said and quickly explained the new developments. The call, McCurdy realized, was a summons for him to return to the motel and he had started the car engine and put the machine into motion before Price could ask for his backup. “I’ll be there in 10 minutes,” he advised. “Don’t do anything without me.”

Price was inclined to take McCurdy’s advice, but reluctant to give Barnes another opportunity to slip away. With the fugitive’s penchant for escape in mind, he quickly dressed, armed himself and left to find the room where, he assumed, Barnes, given the hour, was sound asleep. As he approached room 106, the door opened and a very big man, leather satchel in hand, emerged and turned in his direction. Both men were instantly surprised, but realized in a succeeding instant that their paths had finally crossed. Price would have recognized Barnes anywhere and under any circumstances. He had seen his photographs and read and written his description and other things about him to the point of monotony. But Barnes knew this adversary in an entirely different way. He didn't recognize Price by name, but knew intuitively – perhaps through some sense honed by his desperate experiences – that the man he faced sought his destruction.

Both men, wordless, reacted instinctively to their near collision in the dim, narrow hallway. Barnes turned abruptly and retreated into his room as the door closed and locked behind him. Price heard the lock snap into place as he drew his Glock, held it high and charged the flimsy, metal door. "Hands up," he shouted as he put the full weight of his beefy body behind the flat of his right foot and smashed the door free of its lock.

As the door flew open, Price sailed into the room under the force of his own momentum and tripped over a leg Barnes had extended for that purpose. The detective pitched forward violently as his attacker – with a sharp, well-directed chop to the wrist – sent the Glock flying across the bed and into a far corner. Stunned, Price rolled onto his back to fend off this angry hulk, who was on him in an instant and had his huge hands around the detective's neck.

Looking up, Price could see the underside of Barnes' chin as he futilely tried to loosen the hold that was slowly stunting his breath. He punched at the man's stomach with short, ineffective jabs and managed to raise one leg in an attempt to knee his testicles, also without effect. The raised leg, however, put his backup piece – a hammerless, snubnose revolver in an ankle hoster – within reach and he managed with difficulty to retrieve it and fire a single shot. The .357 magnum cartridge entered the same area of Barnes' chin that Price had just observed and cut a lethal course through his skull. Instantly dead, he fell backward, off Price and landed with a dull thud near the gasping detective, who slowly pulled himself up to a sitting position, his back supported by the bed. Motionless other than his heaving chest, Price stared at the dead man who lay flat on his back, arms outstretched and palms up in a gesture of ultimate surrender.

As the detective sat recovering his breath, Diego Martinez appeared in the doorway and understood at once that his friend was beyond any help he could provide. He had been awakened from a sound sleep in the next room, and had taken time only to pull on his trousers and collect his gun before rushing to the wrecked doorway of room 106. He stood there, gun in hand but arms at his sides and stared at what he had come to believe was inevitable.

Price raised his little gun and pointed it directly at Diego. "Get your ass out of here and do it now," he ordered. Diego had no idea why this man had not shot him, but stuck the gun in his belt and had disappeared by the time McCurdy arrived minutes later. Price had recognized Diego and recalled Diana's intercession on his behalf. He had probably saved her life years earlier and at the very least had shown her a pretty good time. As a result, she had urged Price, if possible, to do him no harm. Price, however, had been motivated by more immediate considerations. He didn't shoot Diego because his senses had been rattled in the struggle and he didn't think he could hit a fuzzy target with the little gun. It was only effective, he figured, at point-blank range. And Diego had a bigger and more accurate weapon that he would surely have used had Price fired at him. The detective had made a split second calculation and it turned out to be the right one.

The death of Toby Barnes led eventually to the resolution of a series of murder investigations, but it would take many months before these cases were closed. Price was able to tie him to the assassinations of Albert Moretti and Fred Quinn as well as the shooting of the young Chicago police officer and the drowning of the attorney, Sonny Spivak. He knew Barnes had killed the two loony Ozark bank robbers in for him a rare instance of justifiable homicide and had surely in the course of his military career separated others from their lives, but he never suspected the full extent of the man's lethal accomplishments. Price knew enough, however, to recognize a criminal when he was confronted with one. The only problem – and it was entirely personal – was that Price had seen in Barnes certain instincts he also saw in himself. He wondered if the differences between them were greater than the similarities. For Price, the question was mainly academic. He lost no sleep over the issue and was mainly pleased he had outlived a man he openly described as "a giant pain in the ass."

"Your killer was also a considerable philanthropist," Diana observed as she sat in a booth at The Bristol Bar and Grill one evening several weeks later with Price and McCurdy. Her reference was to various legal papers found in the satchel Barnes had with him at the time of his death. He had made substantial bequests to his aunt, Sally Crapper, and to the widow of the slain Chicago police officer and to an unborn child in Costa Rica.

"All told," Price replied, "he left several million dollars to those people, but I'd bet my fedora he had many more millions salted away in offshore banks and other foreign accounts that will never see the light of day." He thought for a moment and then continued: "The money itself isn't that interesting, but its whereabouts is an entirely different matter. I'd give a lot to know where it's stashed." It was knowledge that died with Barnes and Price knew it would remain a mystery as far as he was concerned. Fortunately for his peace of mind, he had learned to some extent to live with mysteries.

McCurdy, seated across from Price and Diana, took more than a sip from his bourbon on the rocks. "The man," he said, referring to Barnes, "was surely a bastard, but he had some good points, too."

"He wasn't all bad," Price replied, "but he still needed killing."

The Very End

Other Books By Dave Snyder

Mexican Summer and Other Seasons

A memoir centered in Mexico during the summer of 1950 that recalls earlier events, both personal and historical.

French Spring and Its Aftermath

Still another memoir, this one commencing with a trip to Europe aboard the original Queen Mary in 1951 and continuing through most of the author's life.

The Murderous Dilemma of Bill Price

The introduction of the fictional detective, Bill Price, and his adversary, who are also the central characters in the sequel, "The Deadly Transit of Toby Barnes."